KU-770-703

pocketbooks

Mackerel & Creamola

stories and recipes

Mackerel & Creamola

Ian Stephen

pocketbooks
Morning Star Publications
Polygon
An Tuireann
Taigh Chearsabhagh

2001

Published by:
pocketbooks
Canongate Venture (5), New Street, Edinburgh, EH8 8BH.

Morning Star Publications
Canongate Venture (5), New Street, Edinburgh, EH8 8BH.

Polygon
22 George Square, Edinburgh, EH8 9LF.

An Tuireann
Struan Road, Portree, Isle of Skye, IV51 GEG.

Taigh Chearsabhagh
Lochmaddy, North Uist, Western Isles, HS6 5AA.

Typeset in Minion and Univers.
Artworking and typesetting by Cluny Sheeler.
Design concept by Lucy Richards with Alec Finlay.
Printed and bound by Scotprint, Haddington, East Lothian.

Published with the assistance of grants from the Scottish Arts Council National
Lottery Fund and the Highlands and Islands Enterprise (HI Arts),

A CIP record is available from the British Library.

ISBN 0 7486 6302 9

List of Contents

Editor's Acknowledgements

pocketbooks would like to thank Mike Lloyd, who produced the audio CD, for his sensitive response to the recordings made by Ian at story-telling events around Scotland; Donald Urquhart, for his coastal recipes; Craig Mackay; Olwen Shone; Lucy Richards; Alison Bowden and Emma Darling at Polygon; and the staff at pocketbooks: Ken Cockburn, Mark Lundells, Vicky Hale and Cluny Sheeler.

These stories were developed during a residency at Hotel Chevillon, Grez Sur Loing, France. The author wishes to thank the SAC, National Library of Scotland, Frankie Fewkes and the Hotel Chevillon Foundation. Versions of these stories have been broadcast on Radio Scotland and published in: *Cencrastus*; the *New Edinburgh Review*; *The Green Door* (Belgium); *Northern Light*; *Stand*; and *Waves* (Canada).

Artwork and recorded material were developed during: 'North Sea Expressive Arts', an SAC Lottery-funded combined-arts project, working with Aberdeen City and Aberdeenshire Councils, conceived by Sara Schena, in which the pupils of Walker Road Primary School, Aberdeen, working with Fran Stridgen – special thanks to Rod the filleter and to all the staff of the school; An Lanntair education outreach programme – thanks to Elsie Mitchell and the pupils and head of Cliasmol School. Thanks also to Angeline Ferguson. Ian Stephen's work in the Scottish Maritime Museum was commissioned by North Ayrshire Council, Arts and Cultural Services as part of the Public Art Development programme – thanks to the museum staff, Linda Mallett and Pam So.

The stories are indebted to the oral tradition, especially to two Lewis storytelling masters, Kenny 'Safety' Smith and 'Audy' Mackay, and to the support of Hamish Henderson, George Mackay Brown, Iain Crichton Smith and Norman M. Macdonald.

Sophy Dale
Alec Finlay

For a man so associated with islands and the sea, Ian Stephen first occurs in my memory in a freshwater context: I was looking back upriver on a hot June day on the Spey, to his and his canoeing partners' silhouettes against sparkling waters. Their canoe had lodged sideways on a midstream boulder, they were attempting to push off with their paddles, and his partner, the Australian writer Peter Grant, was pronouncing, "*That's my Lewis boatman: not around the rock, not over the rock, but through the rock!*" – to which Ian's response was a characteristic genial laughter.

A far cry from the world of the sea.

I laughed at Peter's comment because it was so divorced from reality: Ian, to anyone who has met him, is the last person to obdurately persist in the impossible. He is all canniness and negotiation. He has had too much experience of the sea, which would always win, for hapless heroics.

The project of which this memory was a part, SpeyGrian, had brought together a group of artists, writers and scientists for a week to canoe the length of the Spey. Ian and I were part of the team, set up under the enterprising direction of Dr. Joyce Gilbert, a trained scientist with an interest in the arts. The idea was to see what came of such a meeting of various disciplines. The group tried not to become too solemn. One dreich, close, smirry summer night after a long day's canoeing, a pile of us, including Ian and myself, tumbled into the Fiddichside Inn one minute before closing time. It was the kind of night when a lit, warm pub seems an island of humour and laughter in vast dark seas of nothing. Except for a few other passers-through, the place was deserted. The old couple behind the bar looked as if they had been there for centuries, waiting in that little outpost of the cosmos for just such a visit. The barmaid, a feisty lady who could make an insult seem a compliment, after serving us reluctantly with malts from the gantry, required to be entertained. "I'll tell you a story," Ian said, courageously, taking her hand for dramatic effect.

"A love story from Lewis." He began a trial by fire for storytellers, punctuated by the barmaid's "Hurry it up, there's not much happening yet," – a challenge for his improvisational skills. When he finished the story – a romance about two whales in the seas around the Western Isles, – she said, without irony, "That's a lovely story".

Fast forward six weeks. I am putting Ian up overnight. We are to be involved together in a North Ayrshire Council public art project. Ian is to produce a work based at the Maritime Museum in Irvine. I am to document it. He hands me a heavy-duty carrier bag. "Can you keep those overnight in the fridge for me?" I peer inside. A conger eel and a dogfish, queer as aliens, stinking of their otherworld of sea, eyes perpetually open, return my gaze. Ian is to use them to make soup for children as part of the project, which will also involve storytelling. Why the dogfish? I ask. It has two connections, he tells me: the Clyde coast is famous for its dog-fish, and the fish also features in a traditional story in which the Kings of Scotland and Norway, fishing from the same boat, hook the same speci-men – a delicacy – from opposite sides of the deck. And the conger? "Well," Ian says, nodding at the bag, "that dogfish is a bit on the small side. And we're going to be eating the exhibit." He is, only partly, joking.

Humour, storytelling, the sea and boats, and a certain sensual relish for things culinary, improvised with ingredients to hand, as one improvises in the telling of a story according to circumstances, spring to mind when I think of Ian. He is a former coastguard from Lewis, a compact, wiry man with a considerable sense of fun. He often appears wryly amused by most things not of mortal gravity, though never mockingly. A good man, one imagines, to be in a crisis with. (I can hear him laugh-ing at that.) He has an island shrewdness in gauging people, the quick sense of someone able to be fully in the moment, responding rapidly to changing circumstances, as the sea does to alterations of light.

Improvisation, using whatever's to hand, is in his blood. It is partly, perhaps, the island thing. "I love recycling things," he says in his islander's speech, lilting and methodical. Islanders and crofters often become adept at 'making do'. But it is also a question of sensibility. Improvisation as a challenge, recycling as an art, and with nothing inexact about it. I once heard friends from Sutherland laughing about an old man, a mutual acquaintance of theirs with a reputation for eccentric brilliance. His niece, who recounted the story, had asked him what he wanted for breakfast one morning. "Two slices of white bread, please, lightly toasted, sparsely buttered, and of *medium thickness*." They laughed, not unkindly, over that last phrase. During the Irvine project, Ian decided to make sail-battens – which stiffen a sail, as bones support a body – for one of the boats involved, a Dragon sloop, made of Oregon pine. Minimalist poems were to be stencilled on them. The battens were all measured and cut to exact dimensions and, for extra validity, he decided to make them, too, from Oregon Pine.

"Where did you get that?" I asked him.

"It was recycled from the door of an abandoned house which belonged to the archaeologist Erskine Beveridge on the tidal island of Vallay on North Uist," he replied at once. There's a lovely, clean precision about that sentence. All the necessary facts are present; nothing is overdone; it has what Robert Lowell called 'the grace of accuracy'. And of connection, too. A door to an abandoned house becomes a poem-inscribed sail-batten which will stiffen a sail so that a wind, across perhaps two-thousand miles of ocean, can propel a boat: here words, objects and actions are fascinatingly interconnected; they shine together in relationship.

Ian is a sort of scholar of the unclassifiable. While he has none of the air of the pedant, on some occasions an innocent question from me about some aspect of sailing or other would result in a talk of considerable and erudite detail. In this respect, in regard to the sea and boats, he reminds me of naturalists I have known. They are a dying breed in this age of certificated ability, a world in which pieces of paper have to validate our fitness or unfitness for particular situations. I remember one such naturalist, taking an ecology student from Edinburgh University round his home patch in Ayrshire, after a chance meeting one Spring afternoon in the 1970s. The birds were nesting in force. The naturalist showed the student a tawny owl's nest, and the roost of its likely mate, complete with pellets below the tree. He broke one open, and found a rodent's skull; oh yes, this one had been feeding on a short tailed vole a few nights back. See over there? Last year a grey wagtail lined an old blackbird's nest lodged below that railway aqueduct, and laid three eggs. The nest was robbed. And see that old water pump beside the river, near the white ruin? Inside it is a great tit's nest with nine eggs. The bird, he told him, had been sitting for six days.

Ian's depth of knowledge, one feels, is like that naturalist's. While he is highly educated too, one feels he has picked up the most valuable bits of what he knows along the way, pieced his knowledge together out of what's been to hand, recycled it, tested it as he would a tiller. The artistry of pragmatism.

It is also very much a knowledge of place. I once was taken to the creels off Faraid Head in Sutherland by friends in Durness. They knew all the names of the local rocks, still, in Gaelic. The rocks were both their enemies and their friends. Naming them, it was plain, helped them feel a psychological custodianship for the landscape. To hear Ian discourse about the Western Isles and the seas around them is to understand that his own knowledge is similarly rooted – or, rather, anchored.

As a writer, Ian, as Kingsley Amis once said of the poet R. S. Thomas, seems not at all literary. This is far from saying he is artless. His version of the dogfish story here is fascinating. One sees in it, in his treatment of the apprentice, his respect for the unauthenticated, the seemingly-casual, and for knowledge and ability over authority. His stories have a sort of shorthand quality, they short-circuit conventional description for its own sake: the description is always subservient to the action in hand, though often unexpectedly apt, as when he describes rays spilling from behind a cloud as like those on a protractor. These are vignettes to which the reader brings his or her own imagination to fill in the gaps; we are participants, in a sort of echo of Ian's practice when dealing with people. They are relaxed, informal, with a sure feel for the voices and cadences of their narrators. Artistically, Ian takes the world as he finds it; he shows us the unadorned substance of island life, unfiltered or unmediated through, say, an academic viewpoint. In his distance from the academic and the literary, he reminds me of a writer such as Angus Martin of Kintyre: both are mavericks, out on the edge, writing of the world around them. In Ian's case that means the big realities of Lewis, its winds, its distances, and its sea, with the human taking its place among these elements. One gets out of all this the random astonishment of everyday life, the refreshment of it, its queer consolation, as if there were or could be nothing greater nor more amazing.

Norman MacCaig once wrote of one of his crofting friends, "A dictionary of him? Can you imagine it?" Where knowledge of the sea, sailing, fishing, and Lewis life are concerned, one feels the same way about Ian. As a gifted writer too, he makes stories which provide the landlubbers and mainlanders among us with clear windows onto that existence; here are engaging accounts of that maritime and island other-world and its characters, crisply seen by an artist's unexaggerating eye.

Gerry Cambridge

Mackerel & Creamola

Norway and Scotland were very closely linked in the past. They weren't always that friendly but time came when the King of Scotland and the King of Norway decided to hold a meeting, saying enough was enough. All that feuding was taking too much energy altogether. Costing them too much in ships and folk and wood and wealth. So the King of Scotland invites the Norwegian king over, to meet Aberdeenshire way.

The King of Norway isn't that keen on meeting on land so he says the Scottish team can all come aboard his ship. They can all have other vessels standing by. But if they meet that wee bit out to sea they can do a bit of fishing and talk things over in peace. Your waters, my ship, that'd be fair enough, he says.

Fine, says the Scottish monarch who doesn't mind a bit of fishing himself. We'll meet you just off Aberdeen and take a few lines along. The North Sea cod should be running. Aye, says the King of Norway but I get plenty of them at home. What I'd be right keen on getting is a decent dog-fish. I've heard they're grand eating. Sure, sure Scotland says, I've heard they're very keen on them way out west of my land off the Hebrides.

Your Hebrides were mine not so long ago, Norway replies, but we won't start on that one. The idea is we get together and talk things over and see if we can find ways to avoid all this wasteful feuding.

Aye, suits me.

So Norway crosses over and they all meet up as planned. They're way out, clear of the land, in a fine oak ship, with everything neat and tidy. Fair weather. Soon the sails are furled and they put the anchor down to see what's what below on the banks. Everything is very decent like. The Scottish and Norwegian advisers are all mixed up, on board, getting on fine and leaving the high and michty pair to chat a bit as they're both casting their lines over, one on the port, the other the starboard side.

Well, Scotland feels a tug. Waits a second and tightens into the fish. Can't avoid a wee glance over his shoulder to see if Norway's noticed. But he's into a fish as well. They're both trying not to look like they're in a hurry like.

As Scotland is getting his fish near the surface, he's leaning over just dying to see what it is but it's getting harder and harder to pull in the line. Somebody comes to help the king but he's no having that. I'll get this fish in myself, whatever it is.

At the same time the King of Norway is pulling away for all he's worth and getting nothing back for it. Till it looks like every time Scotland gives a pull, from the starboard side of the boat, Norway on the port side nearly takes a nosedive over. When he pulls back, Scotland is dragged up against the gunnel. Neither's giving way so they see-saw back and forth like this for a wee while.

Then Scotland says, slack off Norway, I'll just pull in this line and see what's happened.

No fear, the King of Norway says, you just slack off. This is my fish. Leave this to me.

So things are getting kind of tense. Not just the lines. Folk are casting their eyes towards the Scottish and Norwegian fleets, holding-off not so far away. None of the advisers are wanting to say anything in case they get their heads bitten off.

Then this wee apprentice who's been chavin awa coiling all the ropes pipes up. Why don't you both just lead your lines down to the stern where it's all clear and you can see what's been going on.

They give each other and him dirty looks but do it just the same. Both slack off at the same minute so no-one's losing face as well as fishing line. When they get to the stern there's a big splashing going on. It's a spotted dogfish sure enough. The one they used to call the Kingsfish. Not to be mistaken for the other silver fellow with the piked fins. But this is a hefty Kingsfish, the greater-spotted, near enough the size of the lad who's no backward in coming forward.

You'll need to haul together, to get that one aboard. One, two, three … And Scotland and Norway do as they're told. The writhing fish comes scraping over the side. It's got skin like sandpaper and it'll fair take your own skin from your arm if you don't catch its head and tail together. Hold them so it can't lash out. The boy does that and holds it so they can all see the dogfish has a trickle of blood coming from each side of its wide mouth. A hook at each corner.

So they'll need to cut it in half. But there's nearly another fight as Norway's about to cut it across. Who's getting the head and who's getting the tail. More eating, less mess in the tail bit.

Till the boy just takes his sharp knife from his belt, knocks the dogfish on the head and splits it right down the middle. He cleans off the skin like a glove. Extracts the backbone with hardly a bit of the firm flesh wasted. And Norway and Scotland both get a good clean fillet of firm fish. Everyone aboard is starting to breath right again.

It's the start of a period of peace which is to last for many a year. But it just goes to show you, a quiet fishing trip can go either way. And maybe they'd all have been better off with the apprentice at the helm of both the countries.

You need a heavy bottomed pan
or access to a slow hot plate.
An oven will also do the trick.

Rub in butter or decent marge to
beremeal flour, maybe cut with wheat.
You'll have sieved in the raising agent and salt.
Pour in enough buttermilk to
make a dough, soft under a coat of stoor.
Handle it lightly, it's not like bread
and palm down the round.
Know when to turn it.

Eat it with crowdie but
the proper stuff with a tang like dulse
and the cream of the milk returned to it.

You could have had the *Jubilee* for a song. She still looked stately enough, propped up in a garden, off Perceval Road, in the town. Something in her line, though. You could see that, even with that daft cabin on her – one of those that looks like it might have been made with what was left when you'd your new windows fitted with the Improvement Grant.

A big chunk bitten out of her sternpost, to take the propshaft and a dirty great clover-leaf in phosphor-bronze still there. Make a good candle-holder for someone or some very good fastenings if you could find the heat to melt that down. It was meant for a far bigger boat. You see the *Jubilee* was only twenty-five feet or so, overall. They'd been building the *sgoth* to thirty-three feet, overall twenty-five to the keel but the fishing might have been tailing off already, when the order was placed for her.

Not much left of the rudder. What a beam on her when you stood back to look at the shape of her hull and remember what she'd been like. Yet she still looked sleek – I don't know but maybe a touch of the Norwegian line still there. A load-carrier, though, to take heavy coils and the crew you needed to work them and work the boat herself.

She was built by the Macleods, the Port of Ness family, double-ended, of course. She'd have carried four oars and the dipping lug-sail, barked to tan. She'd to combine speed and stability in the meeting of the two currents, Minch and Atlantic, off the Butt of Lewis.

She'd have been iron-fastened. The galvanising long-gone, the *Jubilee* would have been nail-sick, rust bleeding into timber so the planking would have been a bit dodgy in places, even before she was engined. Nothing against the right engine in the right vessel but she was never built to take the strain of that big flywheel or the vibrations from these cylinders.

Ling, codfish, barn-door skate, even the halibut plentiful in her own day, powered by sail. She set the great-lines. It was a winter fishing with a big salting afterwards, along the rocks, the piers, the geos, making the place a little Newfoundland, Faroes, Labrador, Lofoten. White fish are at their best in the months of the gales. Rich food and high risks

You had to be neat at coming about. Enough way on her to carry you through the wind, while the man forward let go of the tack and the man on the halyard gave enough slack to let the strain off. You could then dip the yard to the other side of the mast and transfer the hook on the halyard block to the other side of the boat. Not forgetting to pass the tack also round the mast, then forward again to secure on the weather bow. Am I going too fast for you? It's maybe no good me talking you through it unless you're doing the business. But you see the mast is only stayed by the tension on that one halyard so when you come about you have to make sure it's already secured on the weather gunnel. That three strands of hemp had to be pulled till they were hard. And the man on the sheet had to keep in touch with the two on the halyard. You couldn't harden the sheet until they'd fully taken the strain and taken a turn. Nothing tied, though. Turns of the halyard and sheet and the slack tidy but everything held so you could let it all go, if you had to. Then the combination of spruce, iron, cotton and hemp would support the mast carrying all that sail. You'd lose your mast and maybe have the vessel over if you had the wind the wrong side of the sail.

But she'd get shifting if you worked as a team. The yard setting well out and up. The sail given out by the man on the sheet-rope till it had a belly as firm as that of the cod you were after. Aye, the man on the sheet had to know what he was about. He was the one to spill the wind when there was that bit too much of it.

You'd to be smarter still at tying in the reefs, so you could present less sail to the rising wind. A steady increase wasn't so bad. Squally stuff or a backing wind – no-one liked that. Worse still if you were having to beat into it, tacking, so the course necessary to make way would appear to be taking you further out from your own harbour wall. Someone would be on the pump, then. The iron handle set into the timber duct would fair send the water out through the one hollow thwart.

You had a rough scone, your own barley in it to strengthen the wheat. It all buttered there in your pocket. You gutted whatever species had given the first blood to that boat and shared out the white liver. Opened your scone. Put in a piece of the liver, closed it and sat on the thing till your own heat went through to melt the salt butter into the liver. You might be happier to take my word for it but I'm telling you, at sea, there, it was the most sustaining thing you could get.

But I'll take you further back to my first memory of that boat. The whole village out. Men wading through the surf to her and us – the older children and the younger women passing the ballast out. A chain of us passing the smooth round boulders, passing them like babies out to the waiting vessel. She'd be ready for the sea, pitched and painted, smelling of treated tackle and straining on the painter the way a young collie is on the leash. But they wouldn't let her go a fathom till the weight was balanced.

They'd drive her hard across the bay to show her pace to us. I was full of ambition, looking to the crew bent over specified tasks. Maybe they were also getting the feel of her and each other again before letting her nose out to the open sea. They didn't do a lot of shouting instructions or anything like that. Still the man on the tiller caught your eye and kept you right. You didn't go moving about, shifting your weight, without being told. The man on the tack, up at the bow would keep a kind of commentary going. What the wind and sea were doing ahead. Still a bit

29

of tide here, against the wind. They're standing up a bit for a while. And remember those on the halyard would just keep the figure-of-eight turns. So they'd be ready to drop the yard a bit, spill wind that way too.

Boats and crews were lost. Often the losses were multiple. The fleet would run before a storm that hadn't been foreseen. Sometimes huddled together and sometimes scattering. The *Sgoth Niseach*, some said, was too low at the stern in a following swell. I don't know. A double-ender has to be better than any boat which offers the bulk of a transom against a breaking sea. Maybe any boat is too low at the stern in certain conditions.

But I had my day in that *sgoth*. That very one, as far as my memory serves me. I think I only had the one season at the winter fishing. What you wanted was to hit fish when there was a light market and high demand. It fell the other way. The fish could be caught but you had great difficulty in getting the price. Maybe wars were going on in the countries that bought cured fish. Maybe that's why I'm still around to tell you all this.

Being wet does no harm to a boat. It's the drying wind when it's ashore, you've got to watch. That's what did for other idle craft at Port of Ness. The boatbuilder went quiet. Only turned out a few small vessels for inshore needs. Maybe you remember the *Bluebird*. She was one of them, at only sixteen feet or so.

But the parish always needed at least one larger, seaworthy vessel, maintained for the yearly harvest at Sula Sgeir. Young of the solan goose are snared, killed, plucked and cured. The townships send their representatives to share in the work. Two or three weeks later, when the boat returns, the parishioners stand in line for their brace. With a season's deep fishing behind me, I sailed to Sula Sgeir.

That would have been in August. Our quarry would have some flesh on their bones by then but still be unable to fly for it. And if you thought it was only sea between Scotland and Iceland, you wouldn't be the only one to make the error.

A surviving community held on for a long time after the monks left North Rona but Sula Sgeir was always for solans and fulmars. And don't you go confusing it with Sule Skerry either. We're talking forty miles NNE Butt of Lewis. Canoeists have gone there, aye, and come back too, with compasses strapped at the level of the waves.

Our compass was kept in a brass-bound box and consulted regularly. There was an allowance for leeway on the way out if we were beating or on a beam reach. As to the set of the tides affecting us, well we'd soon be out in ocean current, steadier under the swells than the eddy close-in to the Butt. If you allowed half a knot, setting NE, you'd be close enough. Closer to land, you'd need to know and work all these eddies. Or else you'd go backwards.

With no lines to check and make ready and no recourse to the oars, there was less of the eye of the skipper. And you had a go at the tack, at the halyard, at the sheet. Even the tiller, to give himself a break but a close eye kept on you. His idea was that if we shared in all the tasks the knowledge was safer and we were safer with it.

Even with visibility closing-in, that course took us right to the cliffs. Someone had to jump for it first. I was young then.

By a system of hauling, using the boat's own tackle, we secured her, off the water, in a geo at Sula Sgeir. We made the stone bothy as comfortable as it could be, renewing turfs as required. We ate together, worked together, took the books together and slept as the habitation permitted. We only counted days to be sure of honouring the Sabbath.

The snares had their effect. Our longer ropes allowed us to crawl over the richest territories. The feathers flew and the carcasses were singed and salted. Our circles of these creatures were monuments which were in keeping with the island. But only until we had constructed the wooden chute and sent the *guga* down to replace the ballast we had tipped from the *sgoth*.

We had taken our quota and we were ready for home. We were now a crew and I could come again. If I couldn't come they would vouch for me, in whatever I did.

It's difficult to leave a place where you've become known.

But Sula Sgeir would only happen once a year. And you've got to see how your own island fits in the rest of the world. A dusty map in a classroom with a mist of chalk didn't do me much good. I used the names of the crew of that *sgoth* more than once before I got my own name as a chippy. As a trade, that was an international currency then.

It took me north of Vancouver Island. Around Prince Rupert, the seas were alive. We set half-salmon as bait to take halibut. Maybe we should have set half a halibut to see what came up.

A woman from our own village passed through. Her man had left our island after weeks of drunken nights. For some reason she wanted him back. Some weeks after, we heard she was home-bound, from the Yukon, with her sober husband on her arm.

And how did I get started on all this?

Yes, it was the *Jubilee*. The surviving *Sgoth Niseach*. I suppose I could have chased after her myself but I'm finished with the seas and don't have the same enthusiasm for steel and oilstone either. I had the plastic windows put in last year. Local manufacture mind. No resurgence after turbot, skate or fluke for me. Shoals are decimated over the banks. You'll find decent cod or ling around the reefs.

Remnants like myself.

But Macleod saw to the restoration. A son of the builder. He's the one who lived in Stornoway and taught Building Science, which I believe is a sense of structure. A good person for that job – I've heard that architects in London, the better ones that is, study boatbuilding from the frames of the *currach* to the canoe-stern of the ring-netter. To instil the dynamics of structure.

The *Jubilee* came back to Port of Ness on a low-loader. There were trainees and assistants but a vessel on that scale needs a guiding hand. Macleod used copper to fasten her but in every other respect she returned to her youth.

The cabin took a toppling. Decking went. New oak was scarfed on to the old so there were no visible lines between the generations of boatbuilding. She was made completely open, as she had originally been. Boats are like people. You find rot where there's no ventilation.

Sawn frames were cut to sit snug on the internal pattern of the planks. She had new thwarts, a new pump, knees and breasthooks, all cut from crooks so the grown grain contributed to her strength.

A sail was ordered to the specified measurements of the dipping-lug and shaded tan but done in a synthetic cloth so it wouldn't rot. A scent of linseed oil around the pier.

I watched her progress. That was my mistake. The press-gang got hold of me to take the helm. I told these young guys I'd take them across the bay once or twice but then they'd have to get themselves organised.

They were keen enough and good enough. Now they just need some-one with a bit of spunk and the same proportion of care. Someone who doesn't have to go proving himself and risking everybody else to do it. He'll take a bit of finding.

The *Jubilee* was dry for a while – does more harm than any engine, as I was saying – and sure enough bloody great shakes opened up in that good larch. I hope they get her sorted in time but it's for someone else to take the helm now.

I hear they're planning to get her back in the water again. They've maybe found someone with a feel for the thing. Someone who'll push them just a bit and has a good sense of the compass and knows his tides.

They still talk about gingerbread
traded while the drovers' haggling went on.
Nourishment leavened:

take one cup of rolled oats
one cup plain flour
less than a cup of muscovados
rub all that with a decent lump of butter

pour one cup of boiling water
on one cup mixed dried fruit
(fig and apricot if you're flush)
with a teaspoon of baking soda.

Add a decent sized egg to the bowl
then stir in the fruit mixture.
Spoon the lot to a greased bread-tin
and bake in a moderate Rayburn
till a skewer comes out dry.

It will taste better if
the Rayburn is the same shade
as the uncooked mixture
and you've left some butter to spread.

and don't forget to ginger
– like I've just done

Dohmnall Chaimbeul

He had a gruff voice, they say. So had my Uncle Roddy who was telling me. He got people laughing, as did my uncle. For all I know he might have told stories about Roddy as Roddy, Ruaraidh, did about Donald, Dohmnall. But my other Uncle Alan told them as well, and my oldman.

Alan said there was a mild bit of blasphemy before he got his phrase out – *a' Thighearna mhor*. More of a God In His Heaven kind of feeling, nothing too threatening to the beliefs of the listener. The oldman said it was like something was stuck in his throat all the time but he'd got used to it. So you got used to it. Some people never got used to Dohmnall.

But my *Seanair* could get on with him, another one who'd his provocative moments. Roddy and Alan both told the one about Seanair and Dohmnall crewing together on the fishing boat. It was a steam-drifter. An East Coast skipper. Berthed in Stornoway as often as anywhere. You'd see all these *Brochers* and *Bucachs* in their Sunday genseys, kept clean and dry all week. All of them in the pews of the church nearest the harbour where the landings were. Not a thing would happen till the early hours of Monday.

Amongst other things, Dohmnall was the cook. One of these people who could do anything he set his mind to. But the concentration to stick to it was another thing. So of course when the nets were shot, *Seanair* and Dohmnall would get going on the new shape of the future. Socialists of course, both of them but when did that ever stop a good going argument. Dohmnall was doing the washing up and it all got kind of heated. So the cook throws the suds from the enamel basin with a bit of a flourish to make a point and the forks, knives, spoons the lot goes over the side.

I'm sorry to say *Seanair* isn't hell of a sympathetic. Let's see you talk your way out of this one. So Dohmnall goes up to the wheelhouse where the skipper has one elbow out, another arm on the helm. Not a man you'd disturb lightly.

A' Thighearna, is a thing lost if you know where it is?

Donald now, dinna you be botherin me. I dinna hae the time for it, if I'm to find the herrin that'll gie us all a crust to share on Friday.

Dohmnall repeated the question.

A richt, a richt. If ye ken whaur a thing is, it jist canna be richt lost.

A' Thighearna, there's nothing to worry about then. All your cutlery is over the side, right over there.

Then it was wartime and a lot of waving of flags. Most people got caught up in it all. Buttons and uniforms. Dohmnall couldn't get quite as worked up as most. The passage of time has swung to his side on that one. Since he was drafted in anyway, he went away with the others. But jumped from regiment to regiment, ship to ship whenever he wanted. If the Air-Force hadn't just been invented by the toffs for themselves he'd have been in there too.

Only once, the police caught up with him. Highlander's Institute, Glasgow. A tattie and herring do. These guys had been on his trail but they only had a name and a reputation to go by. Didn't even have a dog-eared photo. While they were approaching the building and having a look at entrances and exits, a thin plume of smoke was going up, above their eye level. Coming from a stove. Dohmnall's most recent uniform, the Seaforths, was going up into the night.

As the bobbies were going up the stairs they stopped the first man they met. Someone to ask. Excuse me but there widna happen tae be a Donald Campbell, fae the Isle of Lewis up these stairs, ken?

A' Thighearna mhor, the man on the stairs said, Dohmnall Chaimbeul, he was in there just before I left.

They carried on up the stairs and he went on down but one of these cops was turning the phrase over and it hit him as they were about to go through the door. He tapped his mate on the shoulder and they were about to give chase. But no he'd caught them fair and square and that was worth a half-hour start. He wasn't a deserter exactly. That was the nearest they got.

And after it was all over where the hell was all this prosperity they were promised? Jobs, land for all. That's when they took things in hand, the boys who came home, at Coll and Back. They didn't care how viable the big farms would be. They wanted their own bits of ground. Crofters' rights. So they seized them in collective action. And kept them once Lord Leverhulme saw what he was up against.

But Dohmnall, of course had another approach. A decent suit would be the thing to improve his prospects. So he goes into the tailor's, not just anyone, Iain Maciver, on the Bayhead corner and told him not to scrape on the cut or the material. Confidence like that gets work done and it wasn't as if there was a lot of orders on the books. It only took a week and Dohmnall walked out without another thought of paying for it until there was a confrontation.

Parts of Cromwell Street have alleyways or other side exits. But this wasn't one of them. When Dohmnall saw the tailor coming it would have to be full-pelt in retreat or face him head-on. So he stands his ground.

The suit looks well on you, and I'm glad the worry of paying for it isn't bothering you too much.

A' Thighearna, I thought it was enough for one of us to be losing sleep over that.

Better times came and Dohmnall got himself a bike. He even got organised enough to arrange a front light, an Ever Ready working off a dynamo. But he was stopped by an efficient sort of a cop. Afraid I have to point out sir, it's illegal not to display a red light at the rear, after civil twilight.

A' Thighearna mhor, a rear light. I want to see where I'm going. I know where I'm coming from.

And then there was religion. That came the way of Dohmnall as well. But a lot of people don't see the social side of it. He'd follow the Communions, village to village. You'd think all these long coats would look much the same but something about Dohmnall's was recognisable. So the same one was still seen going into the Crit or the Caley. There was no contradiction. But he still took the initiative when he came out of the Royal to bump into an elder of his own church, face to face.

Isn't it a terrible thing that a man in this supposedly modern town of ours has to enter such a place as this to pass his water?

Then there was the one about selling the palm tree. The one about jumping ship with guards all over the town and the quay: *a' Thighearna*, no watch on the graveyard.

Back to my Uncle Roddy and the big laugh under the gruffness. He wanted to write down a few of the travels. Even approached Dohmnall and said he thought it was fair to say he'd had a more interesting life than most. What about having a few of the yarns written down just to share around?

A' Thighearna mhor, you might make your bloody fortune but I'd be spending the rest of my days in the jail.

Take a turn down to Hamburg harbour.
Don't swerve via the Reeperbahn.
You know it's disappointing and there's fish to be eaten.
Allow yourself to be amazed by the caged rabbits,
the freshwater zander, dozy carp.
Note the Seelachs, sizzling, sprinkled with cayenne.
Realise they've probably come from Rockall.

Look for smoked eel, too large to be bony
too small to drip lard.
Eat Fischbrotchen and lick your fingers.

Venture down where inshore boats have tied.
Recognise the timbre of marine diesels.
Fairyman, Westerbeke, familiar Caterpillar.
Ignore the turbot waiting for a chef.
Buy cheap kilos of whole gurnard
knowing that the old guys picked them out
from fifteen species in the box.

Trim the spikes but leave the fish
looking like a fish.
Bake in a crust of seasalt.
They'll open in explanation.

Off the Breasts

All these meetings. The memories among patent-mops, plastic folders. I met the skipper at the sweetie-counter. All roads meet here in December. If you don't see someone out at Marybank, waiting for a tyre or exhaust, you'll see them in the Woolies. I was looking along the presentation boxes for Terry's Spartan. My mother had never gone for soft-centres.

This was F. W. Woolworth, not long before the sign changed to Woolworth and the cheques had to be made out to Woolworth plc. I'm not going to give you a name for the skipper because that's just who he was to Kenny F and me. The round face was even more round. A trace of white stubble coming through the red. I'd first met this man amongst others in a boat chartered for a day's angling. Then again when he bought my oldman's Austin A-40. He put the brush over it with Charlie Morrison's Paint and it did him a couple of years. But that was as far as my thought track went. Do you still go fishing? It was his question, direct, no preliminaries. Sod the smalltalk.

Film cliché numero uno. Pan to marble floor. Floor going wavy. Here we go. Like recovering from amnesia in Hitchcock. We're away. But that's how it was. The shoppers passing us by, other vessels in transit.

Kenny F and me took turns being anchorman and mate. A bristling, bloody rivalry between the pair of us. Usually, I had to say, it was Kenny who was up the pecking order. He was ahead of me in seamanship. A guy who knew what he wanted to do. But we'd work as a team to start the Lister. One on the handle, the other ready to pull over the lever on the first cylinder when she was turning over fast enough. Then the second two recompressed when she was chuntering. Since then, I've never fully trusted an electric start. The skipper gave us the marks once. Then let us argue until we remembered and found anchorage uptide from the pinnacle. Quite a knack in judging the slack so you'd hold but not drift too far down. I learned not to coil that warp, on the way out, but to flake it, end for end, loose so it would run.

All around The Carranoch it's thirty fathoms and then it climbs. Twenty, then eighteen and you're right on it. Abeam the two breasts up on the hill over Loch Erisort, the mark well open on the island and we couldn't wait to get the lines down.

Real Christmas-tree rig, the skipper called Kenny's set of lures. I blame all these angling magazines. Something to be said for hedging your bet between the bigger hook on the bottom and a smaller one on a snood. Might get something interesting half a fathom up. Maybe because the three of us fished a different set of terminal tackle, the box would fill with colours. Twelve species was nothing out of the ordinary and some-time we'd be struggling for names, between our town-English and the skipper's Gaelic. Was a red bream the same as a Norway haddock?

He would often start to sing but composing in English, for our benefit.

If you catch a Balallan Wrasse
You can stick it up your ass . . .

Cuckoo-wrasse had the tropical colours, ballan-wrasse, often larger fish, had a soft shift of shading from kelp-red to a green I haven't seen any-where else. The ling coming up, mottled like pike but a valued fish in our parts. All sure signs you were over the hard ground. Every village in North Lochs would have its own set of marks for the reef. Balallan was further up Loch Erisort, almost inland. Not taken too seriously by guys like our skipper from further down the loch.

All gasping colours, darkening on wrinkled skins as the day went on. The light always seeming to be refracted so it came from the clouds as rays from a protractor. Spreading to link us, over the Carranoch with Loch Erisort and Eilean Calum Chille – St Columba's Isle. If that

Irishman visited half the islands that bear his name, he'd have got around as much as Bonnie Prince Charlie. The Prince's cairn was another of our marks, muddy ground for thornback ray, in his case.

Only a matter of time before the skipper's big rod would go right on over, as far as the water and we'd think he had the bottom and was winding us up. But no, nine times out of ten, a grey slashing conger would come up on his single Scandinavian hook. Mustad. Best forged steel.

But it was one of Kenny's congers that nearly caused a mutiny. If that bloody thing is coming into this boat, I'm leaving it – the skipper's judgment. And I played along. Kenny was getting worked up. Come on, I don't have a wire trace on. Just the thick mono. It's getting frayed. Don't piss about, gaff that eel before we lose it.

I was guided into lifting several of the bottom boards before taking up the gaff. Put them aside in order. As I swung the big black thing in, the skipper took his knife to the thick nylon snood so the whole thing fell into the place prepared for it. He chucked the boards back and sat on them. There was a drumming. But you couldn't risk your fingers near that. He'd stun it, aiming at the spine near the vent, in a minute. That one would be in the salt by tonight. Feed half his own village unless we townies wanted it.

No, you're welcome to it. Kenny was recovering. You have to live at least three cattle-grids out from town to eat salt eel.

Even if none of it's said, sometimes you know it's getting relived. Memories meeting. Passing vessels exchanging courtesies. The skipper was on the same tack, still in the aisle of the shop. I'm sure of it because the voice that came through said how was my pal Kenny F doing.

Hadn't he heard?

He wouldn't be blooming well asking me if he'd heard.

The skipper's language was more subdued these days. I'd heard he was on the tack. Religion usually went along with that. He looked well on it.

I told him Kenny F had blown it.

Blown what?

Blown a good job at the Arnish yard.

The yard out over the harbour Approaches, near the old quarantine buoy. I'd jotted the figures down for the surveyors who prepared the ground. That was one summer job. Next season I'd looked at the smoke from the town side, as they burned the farm cottage and bulldozed the hill behind it. Kept a lot of young guys home. Brought a few travellers back. Jackets and collars in steel for North Sea platforms. Cash to be spent in the shops down town. Accommodation for welding-inspectors.

To be weighed against the loss of the more adventurous townie's Sunday stroll. The pollution of one shore which was thick with horse-mussels. The clappy-doos you see at the Barras in Glasgow. And once when it was blowing too much of a hooly even for us to go out past the light, the skipper took us into Glumaig Bay at Low Water to fill a fishbox with them. First you saw nothing, then you were sensitive to the barnacled black stone that wasn't a stone. You needed a decent knife. Meaty fish, asking for a garlic sauce.

No, Kenny hadn't been a welder. A scaffolder and, the word was, a bloody good one. He had it all planned. A definite share, each week into the boat-account. Sure as Pay As You Earn. He had the keel laid in a yard at Buckie. Small enough to work single-handed, if he had to, big enough to put out in a bit of sea.

So what went wrong ?

The twelve-hour shifts. You could see it coming. First it was only one on the way home, when you knocked off. There were a few places you could tap at the door, whatever the finishing time.

Aye, I used to know a few of these knocks.

Then it was after the night shifts, before you got to your bed. Only a matter of time before there was something in the back-pocket or in the tea-flask.

The skipper only had to give the smallest nod. So it would have come to a head?

In style. They thought he'd gone crazy one night. Nobody realised what he was up to, carrying all these poles outside the main shed. Then someone misses him for a tricky bit where they were welding. Goes out to find this amazing bit of scaffolding, pretty well the full height of the shed. And there's Kenny, out of his box, swaying with a big can of that indelible paint, making this huge mark.

When you stood back it was a big white cross. First they think it's a big Scottish nationalist sign and a lot of guys start cheering till it looks like a war's going to break out. Then somebody think's he's got religion in a big way. Could be that kind of cross.

But the skipper knew what it was the way I'd known what it was, what Kenny was up to, when the story first broke. Our northward mark for the Carranoch Reef was gone, since the old Coastguard aerial at Holm had been shifted. Then the Arnish sheds obscured another bit of local geography. So Kenny had painted a white mark you could see from five miles to seaward. Just what we needed. Only of course some tidy so and so painted over it before we had a chance to test it out properly. And Kenny was down the road. I hadn't seen him for a while.

He'll get his boat another way if he gets off the sauce.

And I could see now how the red in the skipper's face was somehow different, clearer, not broken by small veins. I remembered someone saying he was an Elder now. But he was saying something else. No, I hadn't answered his question, did I still go fishing?

No, not that way, not to sea for a while. But I went to fresh-water. The longer the hike over the moor the better. Maybe that was like enjoying the clearing-up more than the party. But I was a bit that way as well, believe it or not. And himself?

Eels. No, not congers. Fresh-water as well. Like reptiles. No, none of our sea-serpents from the Carannoch. He had a small business, laying traps and fyke-nets in the lochs near home. Then he had a stainless-steel smoker set-up. Got oak chips from the boatyard at Goat Island. They fetched a better price than smoked salmon, these days, with all that farmed stuff about.

He'd seen them often enough, Hamburg or Rotterdam, out on the stalls. About the only thing that stayed in his mind from the blur of all these shore-visits. He'd never eat one himself. If you ever taste one, he said, I hear you get around a bit these days, might be one of mine. You'll need to report back to me, what they taste like.

Take sweet peppers, red ones are fine, orange acceptable.
Hold skins to direct heat – driftwood flame or naked gas.
Turn as they blister. Don't do your own skin at the same time.
Allow them to blacken. Cool slightly then peel.
Some say it's easier if you seal them hot in clingfilm.

Walnut oil stimulates memory.
Crushed garlic releases ripening.
The peppers linger for a full day.

You can sauté shallots with seeded chilli,
to add to the marinade.
These will contribute further remembrance.

Angusina

This is a meeting that took place in Billy Forsyth's. That's a bakery but I went in there for mushrooms. Everything in Prestos or Safeways or whatever the hell Liptons is called these days, was pre-packed in big quantities. Bottom ones gone liquid by the time you reached them. Running away through the drainage holes in the package. Forsyth's hasn't changed much. Don't go looking for that name on the sign though. It never said that. It was always Hugh Matheson's. I never knew him. Maybe the oldman did.

You know how it is, though, you always buy something else and they'd started to do rye bread. But I've got this vice. Maybe you share it, I don't know. Maybe these quirks you hide a bit because you think you're the only one and every other guy is afflicted by the same thing. I can't avoid looking into other people's shopping baskets.

The queue is going down, getting nearer the till and your eyes are in there before you know it. This one had red and green peppers. I was looking for a jar of olives, thinking she was going to make pizza but there wasn't any and no aubergine either, though they'd been on offer, at a price. So it didn't look like ratatouille after all. Maybe some colour for the winter salads. Which tied in with all these mixer-drinks, the ginger-ale and tonic and other things you wouldn't want to drink on their own.

My eyes must have lifted for clues then because the beret caught me. Decent wool, but it was the angle. You can only call it panache. It had to be Angusina. She always had that. My mates couldn't see it. Consorting with her didn't bring bonus points. But something in her touch at the back of your neck, under the revolving reflective ball, with 'Whiter Shade Of Pale' still lingering.

And Fleetwood Mac before the boy Green got fat. Because 'I Need Your Love So Bad'. And the walk to the lane up by the hostel.

Which could get crowded on Disco nights. It wasn't a long walk but there was that one aberration of hers, the platform-soled boots, which made it kind of slow. When she lost her own judgments to the pressures of marketing.

There was also a limit, though, in how fast I could walk, arm around Angusina, towards that lane. You might think twenty-six-inch flares, bought from an advert in *Sounds*, were enough for anybody. No but you could expand them by cutting the side gussets at the outside and sewing in an offcut of something else. A flash of colour to sweep and swirl from the black cotton. Flapping like hell on a course up Church Street.

There was a lot of sighing in the lane. It was a bit distracting hearing other people's noises and wondering how far they were going. But then Angusina's tongue would get past my teeth like it was shoving them out of the way, roots and all and I'd hold her and hug her. I liked her. Her daft wee nose. Her ear lobes out from her curly hair, not the fashion of the day.

I'd see her in Carloway. End of term, everything seems possible. The logistics of getting from town out there. No-one I knew who had a car wanted to go to Carloway in it on a Saturday night. Buses didn't go that way after 5 p.m on the Saturday and didn't come back till the Monday morning. A cab was possible. The poaching-money would have stretched that far. One of my mates, Kenny F, had taken a cab to Brenish. End of the road. Total, no kidding, absolute. Then the girl wouldn't see him. Or her father wouldn't let her see him.

But I'd spent my share of the salmon on Levis Originals. My oldman thought I'd gone daft, sitting in the bath with them on. Shrink to fit. Took me two days to get the dye off the enamel. Then he'd caught me taking the scrubbing brush to them, against the roughcast. First time he'd seen me cleaning anything, he says. Maybe he shouldn't moan.

Should have been a perfect summer. But I was missing Angusina's peppery lips. I still had the taste of them. It was her voice as well. Not giggling. Bantering. There was a way to get out to her territory. We could take a borrowed tent to the fishing but not to a dance. Kenny and me assembled the gear. This was the original bent-nails job. The tent was light enough because there was no flysheet but the six-inch nail-pegs added up to a few pounds. The cooking stove wasn't so bad but the gas cylinder had to be carried on a stick between us.

My uncle Alan dropped us off. It was still the dry season so we shouldn't get any hassle from the estates. Wouldn't be any fish running yet. But just keep the head boys, if anyone asks what you're doing there. Legal right to fish brown trout and all that.

We got sunburnt so we punched each other when one rolled to brush against the other's tender form, in the short night. We caught trout in each of four lochs. Caught so many we had to start releasing them. We'd eaten trout and beans. Trout and stale white bread. Trout and black pudding looked better on the plate, the pink and the mottled brown-black.

But then my rod just stayed over when I hit a fish and it did the running. When she gasped ashore, at last, she was the biggest I'd caught, nudging the two pounds. I faffed about, unhooking her till it was too late. A two pound trout was something to boast about. Then I tried supporting her upright in the clear water till the oxygen could get through her gills. She was too far gone.

There were eagles circling over the high ground, north and south of us. Wide wing tips breaking clear skies. It was Saturday and we rose early. Moved camp by carrying everything back to the road, hitching a lift to the crossroads, near Garynahine. Having one go in the loch over the hill and finding the fish gone poor. Wormed. Well, now we knew.

We were in luck again. Karma was sound. Kudos could have been better, arriving courtesy of Massey-Fergusson. But we got there. Some of these efforts were two-bit jobs, with the accordionist propped against the back-wall and fed occasionally from a half-bottle. But this was a proper dance. They had amplifiers, bass, lead with tremolo echo. I sighted Angusina's pal first. Made a small attempt to get Kenny dancing with her. Then I was in Angusina's smell and her wiry hair was over my burned face. Talk about be gentle with me my darling.

But she was and she led me away from the band who were trying to tell me that my cheating heart would tell on me. Out the door and the weight of Rayburn fume came at you in the calm air. It made the swirling smoke in the concrete hall seem healthy. Always a few collie-dogs slinking by.

We didn't go far. Down a croft, away from the road. Sad day I left it, the croft, not the road. We leaned back against the traditional backrest. My teeth didn't get in her way any more and she went easy on my sunburned neck. She said she'd make it cool. I don't know that she did but her tongue felt all right there. I stopped worrying about the herringbone peat stack pattern getting embossed in my backside. But the mind was racing with what you were supposed to do and supposed to be carrying and the only plastic or nylon in my pocket was a cast of fishing line.

If she was angry with me she didn't show it much. She led me back to her sleeping house. Cut me a doorstep from that morning's loaf, the crust fired black. A slab of Anchor butter and the salt in it eaten with the loaf and another orange slab of Scottish Cheddar. More tea. And whispering talk and more tea on her lips this time, at the door. Not in a big hurry to leave.

Five minutes back to the hall and Kenny F was bristling. He'd delayed, not wanting to see me stranded and our lift was gone. There was one battered Cortina still there. How come they always had crumpled wings? Maybe the only ones allowed to be borrowed for transport to dances like this. Windows were pretty steamed up. Wasn't going nowhere for a while. So we turned heels on Carloway.

Passed the hotel which was dead and the surviving thatched house beside it, which was still full of beans. We came close to calling it a night when we stumbled on a digger left at roadworks, with the sliding door unlocked. Gospel according to JCB. It would have done for one, not for two. We'd broken camp in the Uig hills only that morning and energy was failing. But we were helped by one of the diminishing number of Morris Travellers still on the road. It had come from an even more distant dance than ours. Still in full swing when he'd left. Stamina survives up in the North. Got off with a dame from the wild West Side. He dropped us at our crossroads. Sure we didn't want to go in town? Manyana.

For the first time in my life, town was strange. School went back. Word came from a go-between, older than me, that so-and-so, from the sixth year and also from the same village as Angusina, was interested but only if I considered myself unattached. She had long black hair, dark eyes and everyone thought she was something.

Me – still in the summer clothes of rebellion, with the peace and love patches now sewn on to my new jeans in a pattern you hoped looked random – I had to conform. So I lost Angusina. From some far but still wakeful corner of my daft eyes, I saw her run from the YM hall. I was shuffling around it with my arms full of long black hair. Status smelled good. Until I saw Angusina going for the door. Seized in my tracks. Gone.

Which brings me back to Billy Forsyth's. Her recognising me. We're talking ten years here. Me still reeling, just catching the words. They always had an open house. The sisters were all up as well, for the New Year anyway. I should make it out.

You say these things. Where was she working? Glasgow again. Come back from Israel. All experience. And me?

Settled back in the old town.

Had she time for a coffee, across the road? But there was a car hooting outside, where it shouldn't be parked and she was gathering up the bags and it was my turn to go through the check-out.

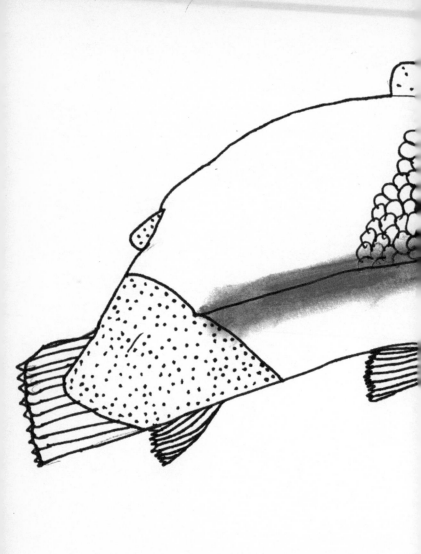

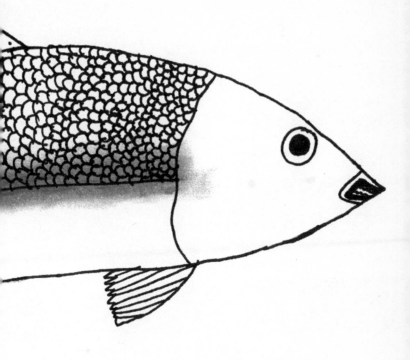

Willack & Lisach
Anna & Mary
Catamaran

First grow some dill and that flattish-bladed Italian parsley. Your patch or box.
Go to a loch a long way from any road a good few days after a decent rainfall.
Leave the fly-rod behind because it will get in the way.
When you've caught enough for the number of people who'll be eating, leave.
You're unlikely to get done for poaching with rod and line but they'll take your fish.

Have a dram and start cooking when you're hungry from the bogslog.
Gut fish, leave heads intact and make several slashes across the thick backs
so the seasoning and butter will enter the pink.
Stuff the cavities with as much parsley and dill, maybe chives as you can fit.
More butter in the cavities as well as in the slits, or olive oil if you'd rather.
Fair turn of pepper. Squeezing of lemon.

A grill at the top of an oven is best so
they're kind of baking as they're browning.
Look for crackling. Turn with care.

Best if there's some new spuds from the aforementioned garden.
You can dribble on the buttery juices from the pan, maybe with a drop
of white wine stirred in but I wouldn't bother doing the cream sauce bit.
More green wouldn't go wrong.

She offered me soup and held out the loaf to me often enough but it was only the once I laid down fish on her boards. The table always had a cover you could wipe easily. You still called it oilcloth but they're not made of that any more. Like a lot of things they've come back into fashion again.

It was a mighty pot, for two people. Still it had to serve them every day and soup was usually the meal. Make no mistake, there wasn't much ritual in the breaking of bread.

She knew the money was well spent on the local loaf. That stuff in the packets, the Bilsland loaf, had come all the way from Glasgow – it had no substance in it. They liked their bread fresh. She put the knife to the crust, rather than just tearing portions off. It was easier for the oldman and the bread went further. But she did seem to weigh you up as she measured the slices and I always got offered a doorstep.

Lisach wouldn't have judged me like that if she'd seen the Sunday dinner I'd shifted. It always seemed to be after a hefty indulgence, I visited there, needing the walk out. You could take a path through the grounds. Then follow the river. Cross the main road and go back a couple of hundred yards, across from the quarry, towards town and there it was. Maybe a hundred yards off the road.

There was a caravan or two around it, in a sort of orbit but I'm talking about the central structure with a gable of poured concrete. A roof in bitumen and a stove pipe, always belching out from the blackened cement.

Another short distance to the town side, but also offset from the main road, was the bungalow. It had green railings around it, set into a roughcast wall. Willack had build it from all the wool-waste and old batteries he'd collected. A house built of tweed-yarn and lead. He'd lived in it, with Lisach, for a year or two and then moved back to the shack with the tarred roof. His son Donald had greater need of it. Everything had to be spotless for these poor bairns, the twins.

And Willack had missed his original house. He was happier back here. Warm as toast. The cooking was done on a Wellstood stove, quite an original one, matt black and squat on four short legs. Fine castings.

Even when I felt bloated, I should never have refused a thing that was offered me there. I could bite my lip at that now.

The oldman was happy if the offer was made but Lisach went further. She wanted to see you eat. She would be the youngest daughter but had double my years, yes and has them still. And she had – yes and still has – one of these faces that are strong looking at twenty but as fine at forty.

In another setting you'd have said she was great at the entertaining and she had worked around the hotels, Oban way mostly. Or Fort William. In the summers. She didn't miss a word or a look of the eye in that room but her knife was never still. Carrots and cabbage, ready chopped to go into the pot in order. She wouldn't have anything going mushy.

At the onions she was an artist, chopping them first one way then, with a single flick to the other. Cleanly. From the board to the hand and in the pot, all in one movement.

I can see it now but it was wasted on me then. I'd sit under the oldman's moustache and take in his tobacco cloud.

I wasn't the only one either. Lisach said she could get mad at her father sometimes. She was stuck to the house. Who wouldn't get fed-up? But she'd met some people, over the years. Folk who just trotted out here to get his yarns. Lisach remembered them all. Big Scott the tailor who'd got involved in that work-in when the jacket factory closed. Why in the name of all that's holy did he go to the Falklands? She got an airmail from a place called Goose Green. He was rounding up sheep on horseback. All right for him, not much of an adventure for the wife and kids, down there. Adrian, the big black man, he was going back to America. Still talking about some other band. Brian who'd done all these drawings, he was in Belgium. They'd all come for Willack's stories.

Willack just breathed on his memories and he was a boy in bare feet. Behind a criss-cross of sad ponies; biting harness. Yes and people who would make the offer, bring you in for tea and them living right next door to others who said tinker as if it was a spit.

I sat on the stool. All Willack said was from the wide chair under the photograph. What a frame that picture had – must have been salvaged from the remains of some Old Master. The Willack in it was too young for more than the hint of a moustache but was all kilted and buckled.

Aye they'd been happy enough to accept the traveller-boy in the army. There was no malice though, in most of the lads, when you were living in the same shit. But I wasn't to listen to any of those who said that war brought people together. Maybe the second one was different but the first was just a mess. I was lucky not to have been around then. It couldn't have been that different for the Germans. What had the Kaiser got to do with these lads. Just another big moustache under a helmet with a spike in it.

Lisach wouldn't intrude when Willack got going but she'd have taken her onion knife to me rather than let me go from their place without taking tea. I'd always drink it to the last drop and was careful not to grimace at the sugary bit towards the bottom. I couldn't tell Lisach I didn't indulge in the white crystals. Tea had sugar and soup had onions. She saw it like that and she wasn't far wrong. What's the difference, sugar in the tea or in the chocolate biscuit I often took with it, at home.

It took a while to see what was in that woman. Yes and still is. And the last few times I was in that house the focus was all on her. The oldman's lungs were going and his voice with them. Lisach could speak out.

My sister, was she still nursing? Good for her. She could go anywhere. And that friend I'd brought from the other island, Shetland wasn't it, he was still trying for his First Mate's. What, him going off with a band as well. And they talk about travellers running away from things. There had to be something in these guitars. Maybe she should have had one herself instead of the melodeon.

Wasn't Africa terrible now, but. The poor people had a hard time of it but the black ones always seemed to get the worst of it.

But she wouldn't hide it from me now. He wasn't well. It hurt him not having his voice. He still liked it if there was some life about the place. People speaking away. He didn't miss much. Was I still working out there, the estate, still with the ponies?

Yes and now I gave them apple cores to bribe them, not sugar. That's what he told me once himself.

I glanced over and his nod shocked me. I'd been talking about him as if he was gone. My chair twisted round then so I could catch his eyes, slow but watching over that bulbous nose – and Lisach's faster eyes, concerned to have everything done right.

They called me 'Boot and Saddle' out there, now. Said I'd been watching too many Westerns. They didn't know it was Willack that was leading me, not John Wayne. But Big John's family were from Ness, weren't they. Just a couple of generations back. Morrisons, they said. I'd disown him myself, after him saying the Vietnam war was a return to patriotism.

But me, I'd be rubbing the Neats Foot Oil to soften the harness so the straps wouldn't chafe. They'd have to go calling me, with the dinner getting cold. What? Aye, they were feeding me all right, even if I didn't show it. Fat of the land.

She didn't like mentioning it, didn't like asking for things but if I could get hold of a decent bit of fish. It was all he would eat.

One thing, now, something more important. A promise I'd to make. Aye. I wasn't to let anyone order me about. She'd seen plenty of that sort at the hotels. Some of them kind as you could get but others thought they'd rented you with their room. Sometimes the women were worst.

Lisach nodded over to the pot, now ready on the stove. He wouldn't even take the thin from the top. That time Lisach and I had a full bowl each.

Next time I was there I jumped from the Land Rover but kept its engines running. I wouldn't keep the boys long. Lisach did smile but it was a strange one as the fish, two sea-trout, came down on the table.

Donald, in from along the road, was sitting with her. He said aye they were beauties all right. She just rose from her chair and steered me in next door. It must have been her own room. The oldman's bed was always in the first room where the stove was. He lay in here now.

She saw my shock and spoke to calm me. Doesn't the oldman look beautiful? She made me touch him, a travellers' custom. The moustache was all combed and spreading right out.

Yes, he looks beautiful, I said.

To cook rice

Wash out the grains of Basmati.
Allow a mugful for two healthy people.
Bring to the boil in plenty salted water.
Stir and simmer until the key moment:
exterior softens, interior remains firm.

Sieve with cold fresh water.
Clean the bottom of the pot and brush with oil.
(Some make a layer of thin sliced potato.)
Place a clean cloth under the tight-fitting lid –
it will absorb moisture
released by slow, even heat.
Some use spacers
improvised from flattened cans
placed to keep the pot above
the damped-down heat-source.

Give it time.

The Mini gave a hiss of breath and stopped dead, three metres from the gangway. Good job I'd got the anti-freeze in early this year for once. Sorry I couldn't get you any closer, girls.

No disrespect to your car, now but how the hell do you get out of it. I didn't have any bother at all getting in.

First one to make a crack about tin-openers doesn't get a lift from me again. Not even when I've got the Jag.

Good training for life, this car of yours, Tawfiq said but Mary told him not to start getting philobloodysofical this time in the morning. What time exactly was it anyway?

I held my hand in front of the dashboard clock which wasn't working anyway. I'm protecting you from yourself and the pursuit of knowledge which is of no use to you if you're going on this ferry.

Mary said they absolutely had to be on this ferry. I said that now they knew the way back. The boat sailed both ways.

Anna said that went for us too. I went to open the boot. It was amazing what you could get in that small hatch.

Tawfiq found the catch on his door – he could never get the hang of it, maybe sitting so low down disorientated him – and got himself out to make a show of putting the seat back so Mary could manage. She stretched her arm to get a pull from Tawfiq.

Help, now, I must have put on a stone. All this social eating.

Anna toppled out first. Finding the catch to lift the seat, driver's side. The tall one. That was emphasised now by the short, snug jacket. She still had a brown roll clenched between her teeth, her hands getting her own bags. All the doors were wide open. The frost had gone from the back screen. Maybe that heating thing was working again or maybe it was just the heat from everybody.

Both Anna and Mary had small, neat backpacks, the new sort without the frame. Tawfiq was out now, gathering a clutch of carrier bags. Mary was yawning, looking out across the harbour.

The gangway had safety rails either side but it was at quite an angle with the big tide. They could stretch out today. There wouldn't be many other people travelling. This time of year you only had to watch it if it was the end of a holiday or the start of the Mod.

End of a holiday for us, Anna said. But a strange time of year to go gallivanting to the Islands.

They stowed their packs while Tawfiq hung on to the bags. Most of the luggage racks, outside the lounge were empty. I said I'd go ahead and scout for a good place. But Anna was saying something. She was leaning against the bulkhead, the longer hair falling down by the white painted rivets.

This island, I have to say, is a bit different from anywhere else I've been.

She tried to travel without expectations but she'd had a few and they'd been way out. Some ways it wasn't so different from Ireland.

I'd stopped trying to organise things and said, hell she'd better whisper that here. This was the Presbyterian not the Papist end of the Hebrides.

No, but Mary agreed. Everyone seemed so quiet at first but then they really let their hair down. People telling you their life stories and that.

Tawfiq said that probably happened to the two of them wherever they went. The girls looked to each other. Maybe there was something in that.

I saw that Tawfiq hadn't shaved for a few days. You're going to have your work cut out there. Back to the office, today.

Anna was taking the bags through. Tawfiq was checking the numbers in his pocket book. He used out-of-date diaries and wrote all across their lines. I wondered how he kept track of business appointments.

Where had this pair been? Yes, it was Mary who'd spent time in Nigeria. She'd been talking about everybody in the village she was working in, getting persuaded to buy tin roofs they didn't need, to replace ones that didn't cost them anything. Same with baby-milk in tins with pictures of white kids smiling. This was the way the modern world was going and their village could be part of it. So many deaths anyway you couldn't relate some at once to the unsterilised teats and bottles.

And Anna in the Navaho Reservation. Not just passing through. She'd shown us the photos. There weren't many of the artifacts, a couple of very fine weavings. It was more, this was so-and-so. I'd get on with that guy – I should meet him sometime. Anna was looking at me now. Had I got the address? A lot of bookshops in Dublin. Plenty always happening but that wasn't the city for her really. It was the jawing, a lot of jawing going on all the time.

Didn't sound too bad.

She was a listener as well as a talker. She had the washed cords on. She looked pretty fit, for an office worker. Maybe into squash. She had good shoes on, decent walking soles but bright-red uppers.

Mary was usually in the long dresses. Fresh-printed and trailing boldly from the straight coat. She didn't talk with the same animation as Anna but she'd surprise you. The hand would come down with a thump on your forearm and just rest there for emphasis until she'd made the point.

We were early. It was me, checking on the time. Wouldn't be the first one to realise too late, that the boat had sailed. Make an unscheduled two-way crossing of the Minch. They said they couldn't extend this trip like they had the last one. Both of them, from different continents, at about the same time, independently working-out the letters back to Ireland. Parents and jobs waiting for them and them both taking another three month extension.

Then Anna with the unplanned stop-over in New York. Tough to face-up to at the time but now it just said it all. On the way home. And Mary too wanting to get out of cities, even Dublin. That experience again. You wanted back there, not for any good you could do, but for yourself.

Tawfiq asked them, both of them now fallen into the way of just leaning a shoulder on that steel, if they didn't think this island was as materialistic as anywhere. The new car for status, parked in the queue outside the church. He saw it all in his job, no names, but all these columns of figures to justify this and that.

Mary said no it wasn't. Anna said it was. But not exactly. A lot of people in clay houses wanted everything as well and you could see their point, sure. They had as much right to all the consumer electronic stuff as anybody else.

And other folk, Africa or North America, made a sure point of choosing everything around them to say what their values were. Not just filling the house with new stuff. Like my father with his patterns, all these things out of his own head. That beautiful wool, the oily smell of it. But now they could just about start a factory themselves, when they got back.

So what were the values, what exactly ?

Jesus, we couldn't get started on this one with the ferry about to sail.

Tawfiq looked at his watch this time. He nodded.

Mary had to say we guys seemed to be pretty organised, as men went. The wholemeal rolls warm from the bakers, at an ungodly hour. Tawfiq's bachelor apartment, bamboo partitions, pot-plants the lot. Its own island in the middle of a town planner's nightmare. And these woven hangings. Like tweed but not exactly tweed. The wool mixed with all sorts of other things and kind of allowed to make its own form. They were beautiful. She could hardly believe a man had designed them. You'd need to be proud of a father like that.

We'd driven, one night, to the road-ends. After a few days in the heart of the town you had to get out there and remind yourself you were on an island. The seams in the cliffs have the same energy as the sea. We'd got there just on dark, at the dips, with Tawfiq having to fight free of a client to get away. But we'd got out for a short venture across that shore. The wind was really getting going and the surf was blown back across the tops. But maybe that wasn't anything new for them. I'd read about their own Atlantic storm-beaches. The strong sea-bass.

Getting to the beaches wasn't a thing they thought of doing much, back in Ireland.

She'd given us a scare, back on the tarmac. Anna had gotten to the car first, taking her big jacket off. Me lingering to nod something to Tawfiq and Mary. Then hearing the engine. Anna finding my keys thrown on the dash and pretending she was pissed-off over something. Driving three hundred yards round the corner, so we were looking to each other and saying, no, she wouldn't. No. But the distance just long enough for the seed of doubt. And her killing herself laughing, like a twelve year old. I recognised the style of humour from somewhere.

Tawfiq's voice came through to me. He'd glanced again at the watch. There wasn't any panic. Just have to watch it. Let's not exaggerate now but we have nine minutes to analyse the secrets of the universe, allowing four to get our asses off this boat.

That's thirteen.

Maybe you should be the accountant, not him.

Mary could sum it up in one. We just had to keep in touch and keep arguing.

I reckoned that would do. Tawfiq said that there was an old Egyptian story about a lion and a jackal which covered it but he'd forgotten it for now. I said thank St Patrick or whoever the patron saint of forgetting was.

Anna said I wasn't going to forget and phone now. She knew enough about writers to know there was small chance of getting two lines on a postcard.

Who was this writer they were working for anyway. Sounded quite a job.

There had been funding from somewhere or other and it was a job-share between her and Mary to type out Zebbie's story. Hollywood days. He'd had a part in *The Grapes Of Wrath* and this was his memoirs really. He was a great guy but he hadn't been keen on both his secretaries going away at the same time. Old Zebbie was kind of conscious of time. But neither of them had wanted to come alone, this trip. Couldn't say why. A couple of years in the city or the couple of years on their own lives. As jobs went though, this was a laugh. Zebbie had been around in his day – well it still was his day as much as anyone else's, sure. He didn't retreat into himself or depend too much on inspiration. Sometimes it was from sheets, written in longhand. They were awful, close written stuff, but sometimes he'd just get going and get dictating. He liked to work steady hours and he'd always be apologising about asking them to retype something he'd rehashed. But he'd get touchy as hell if you just tidied something up a bit while you went along. Bits of it were pretty rough.

He'd know when they'd had enough. Often the pair of them would be there for a while, with one doing secretarial stuff to keep the office going. He'd look directly at them, in turn, weighing them up, then putting a hand out to the tin caddy. He'd boil the kettle and warm the pot and get the tea on, himself. That was his own break, one of his little rituals.

He had his charm, all right. And they'd to get back to him. Even in Dublin, the jobs weren't hanging from the trees in the parks any more.

Tawfiq said they weren't so thick on the heather here either. We made a move. No big hugs. Low-key. Down the gangway. See you.

She fired, second turn of the key.

I don't know about you but I couldn't get any sleep, now I'm on the go. Tawfiq waved back towards the ferry when I turned the Mini on a sixpence. We'd take the last couple of rolls left back to his office, up the road.

Feeding the girls had been a team game. Me getting hold of that bit of fish, hake was it? Baking it with parsley. Sauce of cream with a touch of mustard. Him masterminding the perfect pot of Basmati. Anna proof-reading his report as the pages fell from Mary's steady typewriting. Egyptians, Hebrideans and Irish all kind of liked negotiating transactions.

I reckoned Tawfiq would be in the midst of transactions before too long himself and I didn't mean his finals. For once he didn't say anything. Did a lot of rubbing the growth on the chin. Then it came out.

If he was any good at lying he might have stayed on the boat. A story for the bosses. Shit, that was my department, I could have done that for him, in return for another of these Egyptian lamb stews.

No. Good decision. Long-term view.

What about me?

Me and a long term view, no thanks. I was married to the Olivetti and sustained by the pressure-cooker and occasional visits to my mother's. If I could write my memoirs of one-pot meals, I might get somewhere. Probably been done.

We were up the spiral staircase to the top office. The grey filing cabinet was dead as a drawer in a morgue. There was a pretty good hardwood desk with a leather inlay. One carton of milk, already opened. Might be still alive. As he brought the kettle out to the sink on the landing, I saw the paperback of *Dubliners* on top of some files. Shit, Tawfiq, you'll have to stow that before your clients arrive. Not the right image.

I should beware of stereotypes. A little touch of eccentricity was acceptable, in money matters, as long as you dressed properly. And he produced a little electric iron, a silk tie and a plastic razor, all from the steel drawer.

The milk's off. I'm off too. I'll get some chow for tonight. Take it easy. And listen well, Mr Accountant, I'll be keeping a beady eye on our next couple of phone-bills. Dublin's international-dialling.

That half-crazed grin. Go easy on the pedals.

He put a wedge in at the frame to keep the window up a crack and get some fresh air in. Just after six.

Good that I'd had the plugs and points done. New leads. New distributor cap. Most of the variables. Had to start. Went first turn. Took me out of town, south bound road. Past the quarry. Past Willack's old house. I tried the radio but it was all crackles. The frost was over and I needed the wipers. Ought to be able to organise it so you could get the radio and the wipers going at the same time.

Griddled liver

Go to the same butcher regularly,
even if that's once in a blue moon. Don't go to another.
Ask for decent firm lambs' liver, not sliced too thin.
Brush with olive-oil, pepper, crushed leaves of sage.
Get a cast pan hot, not smoking.
Refer again to the chapter in the long poem, 'Moby Dick'
where the first whale-steak is shown the skillet
from a far end of the ship.
Proceed, inspired.

Catamaran

She was dismantled into her two separate hulls when I saw her first. Deck sections were to be bolted onto strengthened plywood projections from the canoes. Paint lifting off. A few colours, there. Bare softwood exposed, in the slats. Patches of grass sneaked up between timber items. A couple of builders' planks had been under the bits so some air would have flowed around it all. That was something.

The mast was OK, varnish peeling but no signs of the glue, holding its sections, giving way. Rusty wire stays would have to be replaced with stainless ones. The sail-bag was a surprise. *Jeckells* – a decent name – was stamped on the outside and sewn-into the jib and main. Wilkinson said he'd kept the sailing gear in the caravan all through the winter. Then he produced two plywood rudder-blades and connecting bars. All the fittings were stainless. Two basic little paddles. That was the lot. Everything was proper marine-ply. Kite-mark and all. Materials hadn't come cheap.

A plastic bag of rusty bolts and a can of WD40, thrown in? If I had thirty, cash, that would do. He needed the space and he didn't have the time for it, with the wee one now. They used to go out together, the wife and him leaning right out and it went like the clappers. Wee bit wet – but she was always the one up for'ard to absorb the spray. So what the hell.

I bought it with cash scrounged from the Grant. If you didn't drink or smoke you could just about do it. If you know anything about small high-tech cats, forget it now. This was designed to be home-built by a person of average woodworking skills. The boy Wilkinson had done a joinery course and this was his project.

My friend the Iranian was looking inscrutable. He'd long-since changed his business suit for whatever denims and gear were stocked in Lewis Crofters. The car had evaporated pretty quick too. Now it was a one-ton van with a folding seat in the back. This Island does funny things to people. I'd given the Iranian a hand with his home-improvements and he said he'd transport any loads the van could possibly take. Impossible ones would have to be dismantled first. Hulls and mast on the roof rack, the rest inside. It was feasible.

No there was no structural damage, it was just all needing tidying. And she sailed well, Wilkinson said. She was stable with the two hulls and she rode any sea. You had plenty of time to bring her back if she heeled in a squall. They'd had her five or six miles past the lighthouse. The sails like new, they were.

I was thinking of all the times I'd been boatman for him when he was scallop-diving. Hauling the rubber dinghy on and off obscure shores. Keeping the motor idling to follow his air-bubbles. Hauling first the big sack of shellfish, then himself aboard. Watching him go down into unseasonal seas with nothing but supermarket bread and lemon-curd in his guts. I never saw him do any equipment checks. One day you start to think about what you do if the bubbles stop coming.

You'd take a couple of transits to mark the spot. Go hell for leather ashore. No other divers likely to be around. Get to a phone. It would take a while for help to get there. And what would folk do when they got on scene? Police job.

We spat and shook. I unfolded the cash. The three of us loaded sections as planned. The Iranian asked how long I was home for, this time. I said I had two clear weeks and the use of my oldman's weaving shed. He wasn't doing much in it these days. The Iranian had an electric sander. I could borrow it on condition that he didn't have to come out for a sail, when my project was complete.

With the duster round my nostrils, I felt I was really working at something. Hadn't missed any prescribed texts all term. You got lost in all that detail.

In the heat of the job, I only got a clue at progress from the words that came out of my own mouth, at Charlie Morrison's. First I was asking for mixed grades of sanding sheet. Joint-sealing compound. Before everything came in tubes to fit in guns, you bought stuff called Seelastic. It came with a key that squeezed the stuff out but the tube always burst. Primers. Then it was undercoat. Then Yacht Enamel. The guy behind the counter couldn't let that pass. Americas Cup? He boiled milk for coffee on a camping gas stove on the worn maple of the counter. Set a discreet distance away from the kegs of paraffin and methylated spirits.

He got on the step-ladder to dodge the dangling sea-boots and found the tins with the code for that deep shade of green I'd picked from the chart. He was sorry they didn't stock the champagne I'd need next.

I'd to throw all these unread paperbacks into a case, before the paint was dry. She'd be ready when I came home in the Spring. There was a wooden plaque already fixed, for'ard of the mast-step but the word burned-in there was *CYMRU*. A short word but a bit heavy for this boat. I had an idea for her own true name.

I'd heard of the water-horse and could see a mane of spray when the oldman translated it as *An T' Each Uisge*. He wrote out the spelling. *CYMRU* started to look all right, again, for a minute. The oldman told me that guy in Charlie Morrison's was a cheeky so-and-so. Last seen him at a funeral and he says, good age, was he? I says not really, not long past sixty. And how old are you yourself. Sixty-one. Hell, is it worth your while going home?

There was a hint I should have paid more attention too, from Norman, the playwright, next break from studies. With the bulk of his peats cut and fried liver and onions inside us, we went walking where cattle used to graze.

All sheep now. And of course no horses. He remembered horses. There was a still lochan here, very deep, he said. I mentioned my water-horse and he said that no-one who went to sea for a living would call their boat that. The story went that the water-horse would lure a rider onto its back and then dive. But if you didn't mind the story it was a very good image, maybe not so bad for a plunging dinghy.

I was thinking of Wilkinson, plunging deep into grey Loch Erisort or West Loch Tarbert. Norman had another story, though. Another sort of water-horse, deep down there, they said. Often a Henkell would be going home. If they hadn't found a convoy to hit, they'd ditch their bombs as close to Stornoway Airport as they could get. Folk down the village heard the whine and braced themselves. Some said there was vibrations but no explosion. They had expected to see some sort of mark, maybe in the pastures.

Norman was pretty sure it was down there yet. Maybe the mud would preserve the casing or maybe one day the pool would empty up into the air.

I hadn't even gone through the actions of carting books home. Peats done and it was down to buy shackles and cleats. It took me so long to figure out the rigging that I didn't have time to change the nameplate. Maybe just as well. It turned out that one of the Merchantmen was home at the right time. He was through the cadetship, going for the first ticket. Yeah, they'd done sail-training. OK, we'd do it next decent afternoon.

When I'd been having a go at the anarchist tactics at school, making stands on small issues and getting distracted from big ones, he'd quietly dropped Maths and collected Navigation. So we took the sections, one by one, to the sea, on a supermarket trolley. Couldn't get stainless or galvanised bolts but these were well greased. Stepped the mast and tightened the lanyards. There she stood on the grass up from the foreshore. My oldman surveyed her. A fishbox with a sail, he said. But the paint job's all right. Then left us to it. Don't think he could bear to watch.

The Merchantman arrived and the two of us carried her easily to the edge. The rudder arrangement was temperamental.

Hang on, maybe that sheet should go there. He was impressed with the sails. Bent the main to the halyard with a bowline. There was a snap-shackle for the jib.

I paddled out and he got pulling bits of string. The cat started to cut through the water. Hell, she sailed. This thing sails.

No boom – that's what they call loose-footed. Main sets OK without one. It'll be easier to reef. We won't need to shorten sail today but don't be frightened to tie them in. With this set-up, you can soon shake them out. Well hell she goes quite far into the wind. Bit slow in coming through it. Dip a paddle.

That was the only fault he could find. Sometimes you had to gybe or dig the water to bring her round. But without a boom swinging it wasn't an issue. So long as you had sea-room. Watch out for lee shores. The two hulls made her very forgiving. In threes and fours we traversed all the bays before the lighthouse.

Sheet-in now and luff up in the gusts. Just remember to put her nose in if she starts to really dip.

That was my one and only sailing lesson. Sound advice for most boats. Trouble is a cat is different. There's a tendency to accelerate when you point up. You've to bear off, away from the wind to ease the pressure. But he didn't know that then. So neither did I. He offered me a hundred for her when we came back in. I didn't want to sell.

Never managed another sail with the Merchantman. My tutor jumped ship. The word was it happened in style. Talk of a car-chase: cops, customs, immigration. You can blame all these movies. They didn't really throw away the key and it looks like he's going to be back in circulation. I knew yet another guy daft enough to get involved in this kind of sailing.

Kenny F was also influenced by American movies, mainly by Clint. He had good-going desperado stubble when he was fourteen. That and a few extra sensitive teachers encouraged him to leave school early. I skived once or twice to go running and swimming at the Airport beach. Couldn't sit easily behind the glass in June. He kept promising to get a scrambling bike that someone was going to lend us but that never happened. He'd have been MacQueen.

But Kenny could swim and he reckoned he could get into sailing. Only if there was at least a Force 4. Force 5 would suit him better. *An T' Each Uisge* didn't run to foot-straps, let alone trapezes. When the squalls came you clung with your toes to the slats and leaned right out on the sheet. You couldn't spill wind by letting the jib sheet go. You'd have nothing much left to hang onto.

He usually worked the jib while I had the tiller but in a way he was in control. Kind of a disapproving glance if it looked like you were even considering dumping wind by letting the main sheet go. Holding on to the decking with your fingernails instead. I suppose we got away with everything because we had the feel of that beast.

Our big day was out past the port-hand buoy with a southerly creaming in. Coping with it till the varnished *Sonas*, sun off her hull, goes steaming past, fifty-odd foot of heavy displacement MFV. Our deck awash. Is she meant to do this? Don't know. What's the difference anyway you bloody wimp. Your nose is out of the water. What more d'you need?

An T' Each Uisge diving and bringing us down, holding to her back. It seemed a long time but she came up and we were still with her.

The rudders had shaken loose. We recovered them, paddled ashore and got rigged again. A coastguard's nightmare at noon, if they'd spotted us from Holm.

After that, we were easy together, ate and watched a movie. It had to be about our town, *Last Picture Show*. Strange though that Bogdanavich disguised it, setting it in Texas. That's why he had to change the makes of the cars. And changed the story a bit. Our own picture-house closed not long after it showed Jesus Christ Superstar.

My sister was home for a few weeks and was up for a sail. I gave her a crash-course in bringing her weight to the right place at the right time. For once I said we'd borrow lifejackets.

Light airs. I should have known to be suspicious. Full rig up. A seal's head beside us like a Labrador dog. Then it got awkward between the ferry terminal and the two iron perches. I could see a squall funnelling down on us.

She followed the slope instead of shifting her weight to fight it. Quite a hefty girl. I never did give her the pukka briefing. I mean, it's just instinct isn't it?

One hull digging. Our normal sailing practice. I'd time to say it was all right she wouldn't go over before she went over.

Now I know I'd have been better off slackening everything. Sheets away and we'd have been fine. Suppose I was trying to luff up into the wind. These Polynesians didn't know boats are supposed to slow down when you do that. Hell of a nosedive and half a cartwheel. Mast right down into the mud. A few centuries of herring-guts down there, as Norman the playwright said.

I saw that moment of panic in her eyes till she remembered she was wearing the lifejacket. Won't forget it. She got comfortable then, squatting on the upended hull but she wouldn't let me try to right it.

I could make out a little group of people, pointing. A Norwegian ship, in to load herring, lowered a motor lifeboat to us. With us aboard and a tow connected, they pulled *An T' Each Uisge* back, mast to sky. We collected paddles and rudders and I got her safely beached.

First thing my sister said when we had everything tied down was would I take her out again. She wasn't a Jonah. So we sneaked home. Herself was out, not far because there was a pot of soup on. The oldman might be in for a bite. He sometimes did, if we were both at home. So we got changed fast. A lot of laughing. A conspiracy. They never realised what had happened. About the only thing I succeeded in hiding from the oldman. And herself liked to see the best in the adolescent son.

Or maybe that was like so many things, not so many years before. Me sneaking back out to late dances. Crawling back in again. Her letting it slip years later, when the oldman was no longer around, that they'd known all along. Just learned it was better to sit and wait for some tides to turn.

There wasn't any warning. "Cardiac arrest," didn't say much. In the long-run it meant that I got to know my mother a bit better. I suppose it hadn't been necessary before.

I brought a case full of books home when I came back after tidying a few loose ends. The Iranian had flitted to White Horse, Yukon but Wilkinson had got hold of a van. We shifted the cat to a fresh-water loch on the West Side. Maybe I was realising that luck was something you couldn't bank on forever. This was a long loch, with a few shallow areas but most of it navigable for my shallow-drafted water-horse. She wasn't far from the road but concealed in a hollow behind a fallen cairn.

Cormorants would accept it as the sea. Flights of eider and shelduck would land. I let go one day, running before a wind I'd learned not to try to reach across or beat into. Dropped the sail on the deck just as she came on to a soft landing at the far end. Hauled her well up and took the sailbag home. I'd be back when the wind changed.

Next time out, I paddled her back to the normal shore. One of the spars that connected to the tiller-bar needed replacing. I sought out a guy at the wood yard who's another of these people who had to get out of schools to get some learning. The bookshop down the road used to cater for these souls: Calvin to Marx; Krishnamurti to Catallus.

Think back. After Vietnam, you could be excused for thinking the Far East was better red. The great freedom-fighters had seen off Allende but weren't too interested in Pol Pot. China seemed to be making solid, chunky things. As well as missiles to aim over the border.

This guy in the Maoist denims said it had to be larch and cut and planed it to size. No, no charge, it was just a scrap piece. Trouble was it was so good it outweighed the parallel original spar. Wilkinson had used whitewood for that.

But, even out of balance, I was operational again. Could get a lift out as far as the road-end and lug the sailbag and tent to the Loch. Enough provisions supplied by herself to feed a whole crew. Maybe I'd get back to normal eating, out in the open. The ex-hire Blacks of Greenock job doesn't come lightweight. Hit a routine of getting away, usually alone but once or twice I sailed with someone else, the closest I got to other people, that strange year.

All went so fast. Time to get back to Aberdeen, the studies. Get the thing finished. Remember persuading my mother not to get up. A short walk to the quay. The rub of her thick white hair as she held me tight . It was my father's stubbly embrace I remembered. Four in the morning.

That year also through. The finals finished and the inescapable graduation over. At last entering the harbour on the ferry. I set out with a couple of tins of deep blue on a spring day. Got that involved in the job, I failed to notice how the seams were open again. Therefore water had been trapped inside. The glue joint of the mast had now lost its hold and there was localised rot where fittings were screwed-in. I made a half-hearted attempt to take the whole craft apart for repair.

But I'd left it in the open wind with nothing to raise it off the grass and stone. The bolts were a job for a hacksaw. I didn't have one with me. When it comes to wooden boats, there's not many impossible jobs but there's the questions of time and energy. I'd fallen out of touch with Kenny F and the former Merchantman was keeping a low profile in Amsterdam. The Iranian was still in colder climes and the sister had got herself exported. No Scandinavian mariners to bale me out this time. So I went alone with a gallon of paraffin from Charlie Morrison's. Found a number for the Grazings Clerk and told him not to worry. When he saw the flames, they'd be confined to the stones at the edge of the loch.

I camped there for the last time. There wasn't an excuse to get you out there when she was gone. All the crackling settled to a real late heat. To find perspective, place this in its time, let's say a few years before The Wall came down; before the tramplings on Tianammen Square. Before The People's Republic became an excellent trading partner. Before you felt like throwing the box marked 'Made In China' back in the post in all its polystyrene-bolstered bulk. Buy the Taiwanese electronics instead.

Only about two years after my father went. His water-horse had played fair enough by me. She was plunging now, the firing going down, blowing, spreading over the freshwater reefs. And me sitting there, remaining dry.

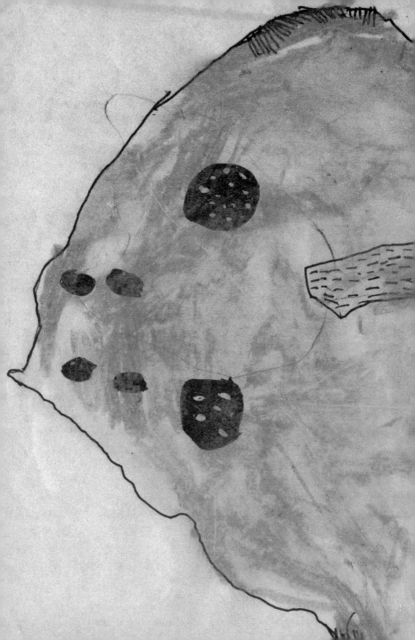

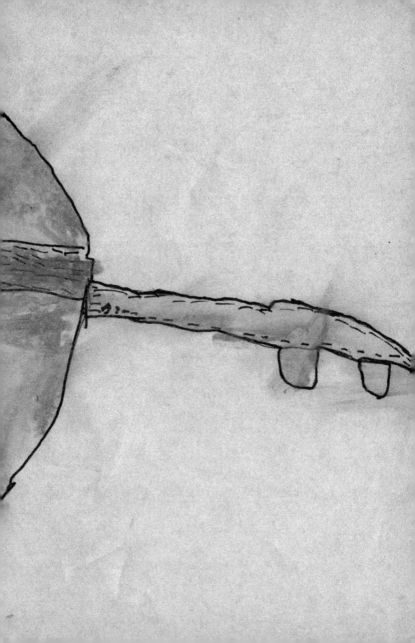

Donald Stewart
Mackerel & Creamola
Up the Lanes
Daniel

Stanley says he could niver get the skirly
jist the way it was done for him as a bairn.
He's tried and tried, frying the ingnions first,
adding this and that but
Sheila says it's the cold black tea,
niver mind the stock,
it's your broon skirly nae the white but
that's what you're wantin.

Donald Stewart

Jock Stewart is a man you don't meet every day.

> *So be easy and free*
> *When you're drinking wi me*
> *I'm a man you don't meet every day*

Donald Stewart's drinking days were over, long gone. Serious drinking needs a bit of time. Donald didn't have much of that with his family troubles. The one fine, healthy, daughter. The younger one who needed an eye kept on her all the time. She'd respond to some things, not to others. No knowing what was going on in her head. Then the twins, the bairns who were alive and nothing more. Couldn't do a thing for themselves. Just lay there. Nothing in their eyes at all. Just needed caring for. Katy had the blender going, all the time, for stuff to feed them like babies. That and washing clothes. That was about it.

He still travelled. In the van, the new white one was a beauty, collecting all the stuff no-one else wanted. A decent living for them. They needed it all.

And now it was me who was doing the travelling. Got the word Donald had been taken to Aberdeen at last to probe his guts. True what they say about cities, you think you've got to know one but you only really knew your own routes. This bus was taking me miles from territory I knew.

That bundle of fruit had something to do with it. I didn't even know if he could eat the stuff but it was easier to make the visit carrying something or other. I'd dithered about looking at grapes, bananas and pears under the lighting designed to bring-up their colours. Down under Union Street in one of these clothes and kitchen-gear stores, which had a thing called a food hall. I'd guessed it was better to avoid citrus things and didn't much feel like offering big Donald a box of chocolates.

There was another avenue to go through, by foot this time, between the bus-stop and the high clock tower of a grey building. A notice-board, placed halfway along the drive, stated visiting times, in white letters, over blue. But I'd phoned up before and said I was from a distance away and couldn't get there in the evening.

Of course I didn't tell them I now had a room in Stonehaven rather than Stornoway. A female voice had smiled over the phone and said of course they would make an exception. The SY twang doesn't do any harm. Most of the time.

March sleet didn't help the mood, following me to the door. That infamous coarse wind, off the sea. Even this far from the town whose main roads all ran near the sea. And everyone thought you'd to be a brass monkey to survive the Hebrides.

Then inside, to a blast of forced heat in the hall and corridors. It was a quiet hospital. Footsteps were exaggerated in this old building. The timber flooring, under the grey lino, acting as a sounding board.

A nurse assisted me, or she might have been a sister, in her epaulets. I forgot to call her that as my father had once warned me. Call every nurse sister, every mate, Captain, every constable, sergeant and you won't go far wrong.

Yes, she said, you must be the exception. And led me to Donald.

You're really from the North aren't you.

Hell no, bit of west there too.

Fruit, yes I think that would be all right. We've all sorts of stomach case in here, you know. Well this is his bed, anyway. We can't seem to keep him in it.

I stayed by it. She would have a look and see if he was down the ward at the television. She was going that way.

There were a lot of bottles around the bedsides here, as in most wards I'd seen.

Most formica tables had an orange-juice and lemon-barley medley. I'd thought of cartons of fruit juice but I'd a vague notion about acids affecting inflamed stomachs. No assortment of syrupy bottles around Donald's bed but that might have been because this specialised treatment could only be had three hundred miles from his family. He'd have been all right anywhere near Inverness. Plenty Stewarts around Dingwall.

No fruit bowl either, only a little shiny dish that was placed so as to be convenient for him to spit into.

Donald came up then, walking slowly but looking as big as ever until he was breathing beside me and I could see it was thick pyjamas and the dressing-gown that were padding him out. His hair was brushed back, as usual. It was very thick for a man in his fifties but all in control. He was as neat as this even in his boiler-suit. Strange that his face seemed smoother, at least under the rough area about his eyes. His grip was limp but he'd never been one for needing to show his strength in a handshake.

We both sat down on the firmness of his bed. Hell, Donald, you'll be a monk when you've slept on this for a week.

Could be longer than that. Maybe I'll get to be one of these boss-man monks, what do you call them, abbots.

Sounded right but I couldn't say I was an expert on monks myself. Think you'll need a bit more round the waist to qualify for that job, though.

I realised too late, it was again the wrong thing to say. Banter's the right stuff, has to be, but there's an element of risk any way you behave.

Thanks boy, though, thanks for coming up.

I told him not to be daft. This should have been earlier in the week and earlier in the day. My sister had sent me word.

Where exactly was that place, I was living now, out from town?

Not that far out. Fifteen miles, more or less south along the coast. When the nurse heard the accent, she thought I'd done the full three hundred. That's likely why they let me in, out of hours.

Bloody wonder they let me in at all if I called that one, Nurse. Thon was the abbot.

Shit. Nearly blew it before I even got right inside. I'll tell her I thought she wasn't nearly fat enough to be in charge.

No, maybe better not. I wasn't to go stirring up the whole place and piss off and leave him to sort it out. But he came out with a bit of a laugh which was his mistake because I saw it hurt him.

Hell, Stonehaven had been his patch all right, whole bloody north of Scotland, East and West coasts had been.

That first truck of mine was filled up with scrap anywhere there was scrap to be had. Early off the mark. But you're not doing that fifteen miles back and forth every day? In to college?

Aye. Well, most days. Last week I skipped a couple of lectures to get my washing done. Fine, only problem was this was the day I'd promised this lecturer, a decent sort of dame, I'd throw in some questions at the end like, to stir the thing, get it going. Came in on Monday and everyone's saying, weren't you the one who was going to ply her with questions, Friday morning? She mentioned that, when she stopped a quarter hour short.

That's it. But my mate and I shared the petrol. He had a Hillman Imp. All these cars you thought were extinct. Guaranteed some student would have one. Might have a lawn turfed on its roof, something like that, but there'd be some machine under it all.

Looking for spares for anything, come to me my boy. Hillman Imp, the future of Scotland. At Linwood, it was to be the new Mini. Thousands queuing up for export. Cylinder-heads kept cracking on the bastards. Maybe they could have sorted it out. Name was gone though. Give a car a bad name and it's finished.

There was a bit of activity around the next bed and we started to keep our voices down.

That poor guy's having a hard time of it. He's like me, can't keep anything down but he's stuck where he is. At least I can piss off down the ward and make a nuisance of myself.

Aye the nurse – the abbot – said something like that. No but the Imp was OK. Except for the day we let the wheel fall off.

Even Donald had only seen that one in the cartoons. How in Hell's name did you let a wheel fall off?

Sheer mechanical talent. Wasn't everyone could manage it. My mate did say, later in the day like, after the AA had been, that he'd heard a rattle he hadn't heard before. That's the Automobile AA, now, not the other one.

You bloody students spending all my taxes, I could believe the first one. And with all that education, you couldn't have stolen one bolt off each of the other wheels and used them to fix the runaway back on?

Finding the runaway took long enough. No but the axle came down with a hell of a scraping. Sounded like a good idea to get it checked.

But both of us were straying to the sounds from a few yards away. They hadn't put the curtains up, all the way round. That man was fair shifting about and his face too. He couldn't ease over to change the way he was lying. A complex arrangement of tubes was taped to his arm. Going from there to surgical bottles, fixed on a stand above head-level.

Shit, I shouldn't be saying it with him lying there, but my own guts are pretty bad right now. Hellish just. They keep setting me a place at the table down there, three times a day but all I can hold on to is my cup of tea. Couldn't get by without my fifteen or twenty cups a day. Plenty milk and sugar in it. Keeps me going. Even the soup ends up in that damned tin bowl.

I'm used enough to spewing up the guts, nothing new there. But what I says to all the doctors is I couldn't care how often they've heard this before, it's being stuck in this one damn building gets me. OK I get to the phone every night, haven't missed a night. But all this damn observation. You wouldn't let a mechanic keep your car for a month without doing anything. If they haven't a clue they might as well just say so. At least if I'm back home I'm chuntering about the place, doing something, whatever the guts are like.

So I says to the whole crowd of them, coming round here the other night, comparing notes. I says now, all respects and that but what's the point of me being here. They've heard it all before, nurses, abbots, docs, consultants. A bit of patience now, Mr Stewart. But I grudge farting about in here if it's no going to do any good. I'm a grafter, whatever else I am.

I knew it, I told him and would never forget it, the day of the barrels. Copper, lead and the brass that nearly killed me. All stuff he'd melted down into these forty-five-gallon oil-drums. Then I'd taken my tea and piece and couple of quid with the rest of the squad. It was the toughest and best day's work of the lot.

You'll be fair ashamed of my college-boy hands, I said, showing them. The blisters had bounced up from only a couple of hours digging, at the weekend. A tattie patch – but quite a long one. I got a good dinner out of it but it was bloody great, after a week in the books. Fair bit of ground, maybe the length of this ward.

That last description hung heavy in the air. Donald had another go at smiling. His eyes were nearly blue, bit of grey in them. I'd never noticed that before. The colour more pronounced against the paleness. A girl in a blue overall went by us making her round. She handed out cups of tea. I got one and said thanks, sister. She was asking the men who took their meals in bed if they wanted white or brown bread with their tea. I asked Donald if he would manage a bit of food with the others at the table up the ward.

Maybe in a wee while, he'd sit with them, up at that table. Don't you be going now till you hear this one. Lean the head over here. We'll have to keep the clampers on the voices, a bit, don't want to go bothering that man there, now.

Just before I left home now, before they flew me down, I had the doctor out again, for the bairns. You know any wee infection or anything like that could be it for them.

He wasn't keen on coming and when he did, he might as well have stayed in his bed. He says I was phoning him up and bothering him a bit too often. Didn't mind if it was a real emergency but this was happening rather often.

Just take a look at these two, I says, and it's always going to be rather often. I didn't swear now, kept the head. It's like this doctor, I says, you get called when the pain on them or on me is something Katy and myself can't handle. Only then. It's not to pass the time of day.

He goes on a bit then. A question of how busy he was, how many others he'd to see. And these words come again, something about hearing the words again – happening rather often.

The regulator went flying off the pipe and I was up and chasing him. You know me now, I wouldn't hurt a fly. Couldn't then if I'd wanted to but he didn't know that. He got running and the next thing is Katy cursing and swearing at me, getting me back into bed. Me getting calmed down, then I hears this sobbing next door. I think, shit – that made me forget the pain for a minute – it's Katy's all worked up now.

So I goes through and she's shaking her sides laughing. The wee ones all settled and her shaking, laughing.

You didn't see what I saw, Donald, she says. That poor man left his bag behind, the doctor's bag, realised it once he was out the door so he comes tiptoeing back here, finger to his mouth, still on tiptoe like and takes his bag and goes back out the same way.

But now the tea was getting underway. I knew enough about hospitals to know it was time to go. Couldn't leave it like that though.

Remember you told me about Loch Uraval, out the Pentland road. Got out there, bit of a walk, out from the third or fourth bridge. One of these beauties on the worm but that wasn't enough. Fish rising so I was desperate to get one on the fly. Kept at it till there was dirty tug and then it gets airborne. Into the side and these wee red spots between the black and chrome. You know what they're like – about as much pink flesh as you can cram into the skin. Not that long but both of them pounders. Anyway it's late so I reckon on going for the straight line to the town crossroads. Never mind the dog-leg back to the Pentland Road. Light's not that great and I seem to be walking for a hell of a long time. I'm getting tired but I stumble on fences and the backs of crofts. What the hell they're doing here I don't know. So I cross at a strainer-post and knock at a back door. I ask this *cailleach* where I am and she says Achmore. She's probably lived on this croft all her life and you know what this educated bastard says, "Are you sure?"

Couldn't accept it. No compass. Moor all looks the same so I've been heading near enough the opposite track. Felt so daft I gave her one of the trout. The other to the driver who gave me a lift in.

He was out there. I could tell. The same guy could sit just blinking once in a blue moon when everyone else was going crazy with the midges. A wee film over the pupils.

I'll leave you to it, Donald. I wouldn't want to fall out with the Abbot.

Nearly went out still holding the carrier bag I hadn't let go of. Some fruit, if it's any good to you. He nodded as I put it on the stand by the bed and backed out. Couple of Uraval brownies would have been a better bet.

This is a two-person game.
Take a barrel to the rocks with you.
Have a bamboo pole with a running line in courlene,
six white feathers, whipped to six new hooks,
sufficient lead to pull the line to an arc.
One casts and jigs to find the shoal, the other
prepares the bucket, knife and rock salt.
Mackerel are unhooked as necks are broken
then split along the backbone, kipper-style,
seawater rinsed, in crystalloid layers.
You depart the rock with a winter's supply but
don't think of doing this until September,
later if it's warm and the dog-days linger.
You don't want to fatten
maggots with your work.

Now, you appreciate all these table football slot-machines with bright figurines, spinning within their set limits. Not a lot of room to move. You had two basic techniques – spin them and keep them spinning or try to use finesse. I think the spinners used to win more.

Original examples are probably as collectible as the jukeboxes of a decade before. That football machine in the foyer of the Union was a beauty. It might still be there, a robust thing. There was also the original Invader of Space. Electronic blips crossed the screen long before computer graphics became better defined. Maybe it's also collectable if it's survived. I could have happily done for it if I thought I could have escaped lynching. We've come a few years from the legendary islander student who emerged at rail heads with a barrel of salt herring or mutton to last him the term. And practised public speaking with a champagne cork in his mouth. On the understanding that, afterwards, formulating vowels without its presence would be a holiday. Never did hear where the champagne came from. Maybe corks were gathered after other people's weddings.

Usually, I wandered into the foyer while my washing was taking its turn down below. This time I was waiting, looking to every opening of the double-doors. I was recognised but not by the person I was waiting for.

The Union was just round the corner from the particular bar where Islanders, both Gaels and Vikings, would congregate. I wasn't drinking then but there were places I would go for an orange-juice, if the company was right. That bar and this Union weren't the places.

Don't often see you hitting the town on a Friday night. Going to the same place we're going?

Could be. I'm meeting Eddie. He's got the tickets. You remember him. Finished last year. Thought you hung-out round the corner?

Bloody bend more like it, his partner said and that was us introduced. She wore the sort of hat you might see a lady journalist under. She was hanging on the arm of his tweed jacket. I was still trying to remember his by-name. You can't go calling people you meet like that the same thing they were called in school. Even without a chic dame alongside. Mind you ... But the guy, who'd been a year ahead of me at school, was parodying himself.

No-one goes there no more. No-one that matters anyway. None of our ain folk as you might say.

This was a couple of years before Bill Douglas brought that phrase back to an intensity it didn't possess this night. But he stressed his accent – a Para Handy effect, for the lady's benefit. He couldn't offer the provincial outlook in an undiluted form.

No idea where this do is. Eddie's landed a teaching job at last. Borders Region. But he's up this way, for the holidays, sniffing out ceilidhs along the way. A network. Gaelic *Partisani* job. You know the sort of do. Scones. Maybe herring. People who've been to the Mod.

Don't think that's the same do we're heading for. And he turned to avert the note of panic that went across her face. You must have heard of Runrig?

Celtic rock-band?

More or less.

Any good?

Great live band.

Don't think I'd listen to a dead one.

You know what I mean. Don't know if I'd sit down to listen to them. But I warn you. This very night, in the depths of the city, the Island students are taking over a big hotel. The amplifiers will be stacked and the wooden dance floor will be creaking. And they will verily invoke every soul, even the imbibers of spirits, to the burning of all remaining vestiges of youthful energy

And unused calories. (The girl's bit.)

Her shirt was tailored and I noticed her voice also had a fainter trace of West Coast in it. Her partner looked by now as if he was already hearing the phantom music, above the space-invaders and whirring footballers. We're off to Runrig. You should come, you know. Steer Eddie that way. Think there were a few tickets left.

The girl gave a parting salute and her companion's final word was something about being sure of finding the right place because there was only a limited set of logical possibilities which meant . . .

That he was already well-oiled.

She'd be bloody freezing, cotton jacket over cotton shirt. Mind you, the padded hat would prevent loss of heat that way and woman, it seemed, did possess better insulation. Now I remembered Runrig. Didn't have an album out yet but I'd heard them on the radio. Even allowing for the live gig thing – hell. Good melody lines, wet lyrics. Big steal from Big Country with these rock-riffs worked-in.

My meeting occurred not many minutes after the Celtic concert-goers disappeared out from the strip-lighting, into the East-coast night. Eddie came in with a grin. Shit, he had a tweed jacket too. But this one put me back off the idea of getting one. The cool Celt's was grey herringbone. This was a wild check, the colour picked up in one hoorova tie. Definitely a present from an auntie.

Big handshakes and I was thinking for the first time that Eddie isn't a very Island like name. That guy who'd just left would have had something to say about its Celtic authenticity. What was his own name again, anyway? Probably John Macleod A B or C. That's how the names appeared on the small squares of the Class Register. I think there were only two in our class. Three Murdo Macdonalds.

With the greetings done I said I was starving and tried to steer the show down Market Street for the traditional Bhuna. Pakistani Sunday dinner, never mind all this red Tandoori fad. Eddie made a pun across languages. Tandoori peat. Fad. Get it?

Bloody languages. I thought I'd given a sidestep to structures of language and got round Old English by going for Applied Linguistics. Had to rote-learn a big section of Transformational Generative Grammar, every Sunday night, ready for Monday. Sure that wasn't what old man Chomsky had in mind when he blew the Behaviourists apart. But my lecturer used to run Marathons. So rated staying-power quite high. There was a famous bit of footage. Commonwealth games in black and white days and him coming in to the stadium, finding reserve energy on the last lap and overtaking for gold. Pity he hadn't become a Commentator.

Eddie had been through the course. Jumped through the hoops and forgotten the grammar. Going for Gaelic. Never make a Gold. Never sing a solo but his choir had done respectably, last Mod. He had a good collection of 78s. Early medalists.

We ate spaghetti, next door to the Union, in some newly opened place. They had an offer of another portion of pasta if you ate all the first. Unwise. Some of these folks wouldn't have eaten anything but a marmalade sandwich since the breakfast that was already paid for. Eddie didn't mind foreign food but not curry. Spaghetti sauce was about right. No spicier than black-pudding, I thought. It all came, Americano, with relishes and a hamburger roll without the hamburger.

We could skip the apple-pie and ice-cream. Eddie was looking at his watch but I wouldn't go until the track on the tape finished. 'Teach Your Children Well'. A better import than the butterscotch milk-shakes that were also on offer.

This wasn't a come when it's warmed-up sort of affair. Some soloists would be there and maybe a piper. We might have missed some good stuff already.

I made one feeble attempt to divert towards the amplified Runrigs. Suppose I must have wanted to do a big ritual sway with my contemporary Highlanders and Islanders. But Eddie produced two yellow tickets and we were on a course. We were as quick walking. A direct route up George Street.

If there's a fiddler, I'll fly there. But Eddie must have sensed I was making an effort. It was a crisp night and people were on the move. Eddie talked about the Mod. I realised it was cold enough for snow. Put up the collar of the cord jacket. Then I was being led through revolving doors. The receptionist said which of the evening's functions was the ceilidh. There wasn't any sound of music or dancing. More taped tracks, C & W, from some lounge we passed by. Eddie handed our tickets to a man in a kilt, sitting with a biscuit-tin at the door. We'd catch all the second-half.

His relative had kept two seats at one long table. She looked good, even under the harsh lighting. Her tartan skirt went all the way to the parquet floor. Trust you to know when the tea's coming. Yes, we have met. You might as well sit with us, boys, there's not much younger blood around tonight, I'm afraid.

No-one said grace. The waitresses were having a job seeing that all the scattered people had tea. It was little sandwiches that appeared, crusts off. No scones. The men were painfully outnumbered. Most of them had tweed ties on. About half had kilts. They would be the ones who went to Mods.

I saw a lot of this crowd at Oban. Best Mod I've been at yet. Dammit, I wish I'd brought my kilt up with me.

I'm glad you didn't. The neck was going slack on my lambswool polo, the one with the grey fleck. I said it but I wouldn't have minded. In one way I was fascinated and alert but, in another way, distant from everything that was going on in this long room. The witty Gael and his lady in the hat would have broken sweat by now.

One tone was quietly gaining a hold of everyone at this table. A bass voice with a Southern Isles accent, maybe rubbed by a number of Mainland years. It came from a man whose chair was pushed back a little further from the board. His white hair was brushed back behind his ears. The black brogues, functional rather than dress ones, were jutting from the stretched-out legs.

An aunty of mine, while the Communions were on . . .

I was warm now but realised that I'd made a shudder. This would be right up Eddie's street. But the steady voice got a hold of me.

The Communions. From the outside it looks like real laugh a minute stuff. Dragging on for weeks, village to village, all churches holding their services at staggered times. But that's only to allow everyone the chance to travel around and have a go at the lot. You'd to unearth the camp-beds. Maybe these inflatable mattresses. Borrow plenty of bedding. Take a couple of gigots and shoulders from the freezer.

Cooking up dinners, ready for invasions. But you couldn't repel them so you fed them. You could never be sure how many would appear. So this woman had the full roast dinners, the soup, the puddings, cakes and shortbread out for three nights running. No-one came and things were winding-down so she didn't bother the next night. She'd just put two salt mackerel on to boil for herself when she looked out the window.

Here they were, one after another, hungry after all that good religion. If two fish was all she had left in the house, they would have to do.

All these sliced pan loaves gone too stale to serve, thrown to the hens but she remembered some packets of that instant potato. And plenty of milk so she made a big pudding to clinch the miracle. A broth-pan full of Creamola but she was that harassed going next door, organising tea, that some of it came bubbling over the top like science-fiction. The feeding of fifteen souls with two mackerel, a packet of Smash and several sachets of Creamola.

Then there was a shushing all round. All the tables fell silent. I was taken along with Eddie, his presentable elder cousin, her reserved husband, the storyteller and the whole assembled congregation. They'd persuaded the medalist to sing another song.

A slight man in a dark suit put his head back and hit the notes. A tenor but no fiddly bits. Solid rhythms and phrasing. A strange pattern of stops, difficult to predict. Then, all conscious observation was gone. We were all away. In orbit.

A momentary pause of respect on the drawing-in of that song, a boat coming alongside a pier, before everyone gave way to clapping. Calling for another. The man nodded but didn't put his head back this time and his voice came lighter. I heard myself sigh, stopped it and glanced round to make sure no-one had noticed. This was a neutered example. Middle of the road.

This was Creamola after mackerel. You couldn't lap it up but you could take a spoon to it, in company with Eddie and everyone else. You could now accept it all, even the second song, because of the first. All in this room with its fluorescent curtains. Where the mackerel were on offer.

To make decent tea:

Have a stove.
If you don't, have the ring of a cooker on low heat. (Solid electric is best.)
Warm the metal teapot. Put in plenty of tea/tea bags.
Pour the water while it's steaming and stir well.
Keep talking while you're stirring.
Put on the heat to simmer. Still keep talking.
Leave it a while and keep talking. (Best if the pot is for more than one.)
Don't think of taking it without milk. Just look at the cups of those who do.

Variation

If on a working boat take all the steps as above but
when you've drunk your tea
top up the pot with more tea and boiling water
(don't empty till you have to)
and return to the heat so it's ready for the next one.
Consider using shakey-milk (Nestlés Ideal or Carnation).
UHT is fine.

Up the Lanes

His white bristles stood out from red cheeks. He'd stopped the van for me at the edge of the dual carriageway. This was not a main-road type of face. He said the name of the nearest village to where he was bound and asked if it was any good to me. I said anywhere past the suburbs would be a help.

The woman turned round from the front seat. She had hair, mostly gone grey, that was too long for her. She was hiding behind it but she said they could take me round, a bit of a detour, then drop me out the main road a bit.

We went on, still on the tarmac but there was a green division instead of a white line up the road. Our wheels took up the whole width.

I told him how good it was to see ripening fields after all the railings and chip-shops but he said nothing back. Her head was still turned halfway round to me but it went down and her hair seemed to thicken over her face. She said they were farm hands that moved around with the work, like. Or they used to at least.

I was away with Tess of the D'Urbervilles wondering how folk coped with that kind of exposed life, long-term. I didn't find any words to put this to them. That was just as well. After a while he spoke and something in the tone of his voice stilled me. They didn't travel much these days, to follow the jobs. What bloody jobs? The East Coast had been the place for work, even in winter. Plenty cattle there. Oatfields for the beasts, barley for the distilleries. Then he stopped dead in his talk and pulled up the van. I would have a cup of tea with them before he put me on my road. He'd see me back to the dual carriageway a good bit before the south bus. So I could try for a lift first.

Even now that the grass was taking over completely from the surface of the lane, I couldn't go wrong in accepting the offer. Except in saying how the stone walls of this house looked pretty solid.

She said it was a down-and-out-house. He said the walls were rotten.

I kept my gob shut but remember, I was reading Hardy at the time. So the echo went by like a shadow. The rotten rose is ripped from the wall.

They'd worked on this same bit of land for a good few seasons now. They were both past it for following harvests.

Sit yourself down.

Empty dog-food cans did as ashtrays on a formica-top table. The dogs themselves were lying about and quiet. A friendly enough pair of collies crossed with something else.

My chair was at the table by the window. A few rows of potatoes reaching out near the rough hedge. This would be their own patch. The shaws had been lifted to about halfway along.

He told me the tea was brewed and there was no show in this establishment and I told him as I laid hands on the cup, I was glad of that. I hadn't realised my fingers had got so cold.

The woman fed the dogs. Then she leaned over the back of her man's chair. She was looking down the columns. He'd opened out today's paper.

Job, jobs, they said. I looked again to the window and asked if the corn over on the other side of the hedge was ripening fine. He said it was sold along with the rest of the farm. The young lad, the owner of this place had gone bust.

No dungarees ever on him, she said, no like his faither. And the cars. You widna believe the flashy things he drove and wrecked in the space o a year.

It was time to leave the lanes. These folk wouldn't be around them much longer either.

She'd settled into her chair when I left. I said the tea had been good and strong. That was fine.

He drove me round from the grassy lane, back to clear tarmac and up to the South road. We went through a quiet patch before I asked how he would cope.

A cooncil hoose widna be sae bad. The toon'd be a right. Human animal's the most adaptable beast o the lot.

I found myself grasping for his hand to shake. My knuckles touched his wrist, bare below his sleeve. It was as fuzzy as his face. As the lane we'd left. I clasped it and he took mine and that was it.

Student-soup is really for keeping them alive.
Eat them only as a final resort.
Root vegetables are the answer unless they're fashionable.
So neeps might be better than Jerusalem artichokes.
But don't economise on the oil by
using   (a) left-overs from the chip-pan
               (b) spreading grease, so bad that even students abandon it.
So the slick of olive or sesame is warming
as you're grating potato, beetroot and the rest.
Avoid fingernails and blood even if you think
they might be a source of calcium and protein.
Finely chop the whites of leeks, retain the green.
Gently sweat all the veg. I'd say brown it but
you won't see anything in all that red.
Add stock if you've got it.
Otherwise turn to bouillon; tamari,
something for body. Tomato, puree or sun-dried.
Lemon/lemon-grass/ lime to balance
the sugar in the beet. Something peppery.
But go easy on the tabasco.
If you know any Polish Catholic insomniacs
ask them around for a test-drive.
Don't eat them either.
If there's an art-student in the house,
serve the borscht in retro china on an old but clean white cloth,
garnished with a swirl of soured cream
and finished as ever with green on the scarlet.

Daniel

Daniel was a restless body. We first met when he stopped the van for me. It was the south-bound road from Aberdeen, just beyond the second bridge over the Dee. Glowing street lamps were coming up on the outlying housing schemes, fighting with the last natural light left in the sky.

I saw a dark head nod to acknowledge my stretched-out arm. A ten-hundredweight van drew-up, a hundred yards on. I went for it and he leaned across to see to the catch on the passenger door. I was lifted away from exhaust-fumes and the noise of accelerating engines. Everybody eager to get out of town.

Just as far as Stonehaven. Aye, that was all the baggage. The canvas haversack. Better known as the piece-bag. He was Daniel. The thick beard was absolutely black. The short hair at both sides of his head, too, but almost completely bald in the middle. I was of course at the University?

True, in that I made it to seminars more often than not. You had to pick and choose lectures a bit if you were going to stay in touch with the music scene. If you'd had a session up some lane you'd never find again, somebody's cottage, you could write-off the next day. That was even without drinking anything. No, I didn't have an instrument. A lot of my mates were musicians. I sometimes told stories. To chip-in a piece.

Daniel wanted to hear more about the music scene out of town.

There was always a guitar or two, couple of whistles, somebody or other with a bodhran if you were out of luck. A decent fiddler if you were very lucky. All amongst floor cushions or leaning back on polythene tubs of wholefoods.

Always a bit strange coming from that back to the Course. No, it was literature. Some of the seminars were good, couple of the lectures. But folk were starting to spot topics for exams – just like doing your Highers again. What you thought you'd got away from.

Yes, I did use the big library. Just soaked up the atmosphere. Looked for the individual carver's mark on each chair, a climbing mouse, placed somewhere different each time. Nice bits of oak. OK I'd look out for him.

He didn't see much of the light. Down spiral staircases and through partitions till you came to his archives. I'd need a ticket to visit him.

And he told me what to ask for. Daniel also told me I was right not to have too single-minded an aim. Anything you did, you had to allow yourself to pause and pick the berries among the whins along the way.

He was a lyrical man. He proved it before we stopped at the Bridge of Cowie. With very little warning, he tilted his head back and started to sing, letting the van take the bends on its own. His eyes narrowed and his consciousness was drifting off somewhere else.

Part of me was away with him but another part was looking at the bends downhill. We made it and Daniel finished the last verse, with the wheels up on the pavement. A muckle sang. What could we say? He was off, driving with one hand, holding the other up in the air till he was through the town, out of sight.

That blue Beagle van came back into my life the very next day. I was heading back into the city. I'd timed it just wrong, right between buses and thought I'd maybe give this a try. Should have stayed-put, right at the bridge before the traffic gained speed but it was another clear day. I was halfway up the hill, looking towards a parked oil-rig, before I thought that no-one in their right mind would stop here. Daniel stopped.

The engine stalled as I got in. There were vehicles coming behind us, climbing that hill. Daniel was sweating, a belted tweed jacket tight on him, while he was turning the key. I helped by saying, count three. He did and then the engine fired. Somebody hooted at us but nobody tried to overtake, without a view of the oncoming traffic. This could be a dangerous road.

Like a lot of ballad singers, Daniel carried a bit of weight. Some people look comfortable with it but he didn't. Not a squash player and if he'd been a swimmer I would have seen him amongst the regulars in the pool beside the library.

It was good of him to stop. The odds against the timing being right again were pretty high. No, not the van, though it could be out right enough. I'd meant our meeting on the road on the return trip. No sessions this time. I was bound for the library. A deadline gone and I'd run out of excuses. I used to have these things done on time. Occasional Alphas. Reading schedules. But I was still getting by.

Sounded to Daniel like I might be getting more out of my education now but he'd got a Third so maybe I shouldn't listen. Mind you, nobody asked what you'd got if it was a job you were after rather than a career.

Sounded to me like we just had to meet. He didn't sing this time. He opened the second button of the Viyella shirt at the next lights. Twisted his tie further loose. Did I know anything about Bedford vans? Mind your head on the table-leg.

I knew they didn't usually have gate-leg tables in the back. This was the largest piece but there were some smaller items that looked like mahogany and two or three painted items – a corner cabinet and something else.

He was trying to make the step from junk-shop to antique emporium but it would help if the bloody van was more consistent. Kangaroo petrol. Did I know any tricks?

I knew to keep the wheel-nuts tight, on the Stonehaven road. And to go for the easiest options first. Fuel filter before fuel-pump, that sort of thing.

He pulled over on the forecourt of a garage and I found the fuel-filter. It was disgusting. I had a pound note handy and it was enough for the replacement from the filling-station. I pulled out the ends of the rubber pipe, one by one without spilling too much. Remembered to look for the arrow which showed the direction of flow.

He was indebted. No he was still in credit for that song. And I was that bloody pleased with myself. Not often these things worked out for me. It was somehow easier to be objective if it was someone else's problem.

Daniel had another problem. He told me it over lunch. The absolute least he could do was to feed the starving student. Then we'd throw these things in the shop and he'd drive us to the library. I'd go up to these tables, set before the stained windows and he'd go down to the depths of archival obsession.

He was a Technical Author. That meant he wrote text for books on subjects he knew nothing about. But there was another book which was his own baby.

He was cleaning a lettuce to go with the tins of ravioli and beans. I knew not to try to move the papers, photos and captions that were laid like tiles of lino, over the carpet in the dining room. I knew organisation when I saw it. But there was another research project, he meant, apart from his book of Old Photographs and whatever was on the stocks for Aberdeen University Press. His last book of Old Photographs was Plymouth. He'd grown up there, was schooled not so far from there. Met his wife not so far from there.

But now he'd traced a connection. He'd been adopted. That hadn't really been a secret. Now it was important for him to trace the lines back. That ballad was part of it. So it was from the southwest of England to the northeast of Scotland. He told me more as we ate on the hoof.

Then placed the furniture, without obvious mishap, into a shop, round the corner. The glass door was open. A joiner was cutting board on trestles inside.

His family had been Travellers. Some were now settled in this city. There were some superb singers and musicians.

I wasn't going to get all my notes down by evening and I'd be kidding myself if I brought the books home to add to the pile. I'd have to do some more at the library so it wasn't worth while going back out of town. It was an evening to stay on an island. There was one, a house due for demolition, still very much alive amongst the levelled ones around it, up from the nearest thing the city had to flyovers. Where the big traffic filtered down to the harbour. Near where bolted timber doors, bigger than barn-doors, said 'Shore Porters Society', which sounded more strange than an Aberdeen version of Pickfords. Another West Coast refugee had a room in the high island. A temporary lease. There was a chimney which still worked. Plenty of wood on the waste ground and still more at the beach beside Cordona's Funfair.

I went to his island and he told me of the family bakers' shop. He was writing a story. He got angry when I picked at some bread and said I should eat if I was hungry. He cut the loaf in two. His folks were in the Black Isle now. No he couldn't see himself going back to the West Coast. All run-down. The NATO fuel-jetty was at Aultbea. Jobs meant dependence, Nigg or NATO and subject to international markets and politics the both of them.

The girl from next door came through and brought a bucket of coal. She was going to stay up tonight. She was a drama student but there was a written piece of work to complete. Angus said maybe she was in luck, this was a literature student.

It was on Pinter. I said I knew a bit about *The Caretaker* and this seemed the right place to write about it. Displaced persons. So long as we didn't start fighting about the pecking order.

The other Coast-Wester knew a bit about *The Birthday Party* and he'd had a walk-on part in *The Visit* by Durenematt, who was arguably a kind of Swiss Pinter. Hell, I'd seen it. Yes he was one of the guys in the long leather coats.

Shit, we had a thesis, to run with. We wrote her essay together, all three of us talking fast and her typing like crazy. When it was done, nobody went to bed because she spoke of Venezuela. Some beautiful music.

Shit, did she look Venezuelan? No she'd grown up in Edinburgh. Her Dad was a diplomat.

We did get her to sing, though and I saw the Spanish drifting with the smoke from our chimney over a city that was just waking up.

We went for rolls, crossing the wide road on a steel-sided bridge.

I drifted through a lecture that morning but also sought-out Daniel, down in the depths of the library. He was a fixture here. Had access to a kettle. Go on, don't need a spoon – give a big shake from the jar into these cups. Take a look at these. And I was into the shadows, the reflections in the puddles in the hollows of the cobbles. Somebody had been passing by just then. Faster than the shutter-speed. Maybe they'd had children. Maybe they were living in Aberdeen. Or Plymouth. Or Venezuela. Did I know a lot of displaced children were shipped from Aberdeen? Not very far from the Shore Porters was a warehouse which had been last stop, before the Colonies.

Daniel had had a breakthrough. The real research, tracing his own parentage, had gone as if his life depended on it. Now he was certain. All the clues led to places within a couple of hours travel from this very city. Even the housing estates on the outskirts. It looked like people would see him. And if I was coming into Aberdeen this weekend, there was a few people coming round to Whitehall Road. Nothing fancy. Baked potatoes, sort of thing. Any other musicians?

OK, sounded good but I'd need to sleep till then. Navigated my way back up towards the light. Pretty fair imitation of a mole. Remembering the war my Broch Grampa waged against these beasts. Thought of the traps every time the word moleskin came up. Back to ground-floor level, I realised someone else was talking to me.

If I hadn't been so bloody dozy, I'd have asked her to Daniel's do. She came after me to see how it was going. Maybe she was a bit worried watching me trying to get across the road on automatic pilot. No old ladies handy to give me a hand.

I told her to enjoy herself this year. Final year was crap. Question roulette. Planning essays to fit the bill.

Afterwards? The Hebrides?

Yes, I'd probably go back.

She really envied me, that. Everyone looked at her and saw a black girl, pretty rare up here. Till she started to speak, everyone thought she must have good ethnic roots. Or issues at least. But she felt she was only ebonised.

I looked closely at her skin and wanted to make a moist touch, to make sure. Maria was stunning. Cropped tight hair, dead slim. Very graceful. She was also very Oxford. Or somewhere. She said, nowhere. It was after I went to get the bus I thought she would have come to Daniel's place. Sounded like this session was what she was looking for. Maybe she was just one displaced person too many, that week.

Daniel's book was back from the printers. What I'd witnessed the other day had been the final layout. The book-launch and all that was still to come. This was just letting the hair down. Some friends I'd to meet.

I was sure the first guy had to be one of Daniel's long lost relatives. He had sprouting black ringlets and wore a tailcoat. Sure enough, there was a pair of trainers rather than patent leather shoes underneath it all. They were now giving all they had to give on the great brass pedals of an upright piano which was interrupting Daniel's hall. It was a name you'd heard of but wasn't quite in tune.

When the player stopped, to say something to me, he was from Welsh Wales. I was about to say he was a red herring but he was introducing himself as Gareth. But one who had absolutely no interest in Rugby, best to kill that one before it tried to start. Not that the accidental circumstances of one's birth mattered a toss anyway. Had I been invited by Daniel, not that it mattered much, either?

It looked like Daniel was our mutual friend.

Not another bloody student of Literature. Was nobody studying anything useful these days?

Like?

Agriculture.

Over-production.

What of? Agricultural students?

Agricultural products. I'd bitten.

Dressed like that, I thought it might be brandy but no it was a half-bottle of whisky on top of the piano. A change from the normal Lambrusco.

No, I'd away and boil the kettle. Looked like there might be a session, getting going.

A Victorian wardrobe that was too big to shift again and was no longer needed because it's entire contents had gone to the printers, was being sacrificed. I said that some boring people just put potatoes into the oven. It blazed high. I noticed that among the people coming and going, there didn't seem to be any of Daniel's neighbours hopping over the fence to join in.

I caught a glimpse of Daniel, then. He was tearing off bits of celery to liven up a catering pack of tomato soup. He still managed to signal something across. Aye, sure. I'd be up for a story later. Things would quieten down when the fire went low.

Recognised the particular wardrobe from a few broken panels that were waiting to be fed to the flames. I'd eaten part of my lunch, a salad, off it, that second day with Daniel. It had better be said that it was on its side at the time though I could easily imagine Daniel eating spaghetti hoops while sitting on the top of one.

Gareth's voice was in my ear again. He'd always wanted to go to bed with George Eliot? And this was the nearest he was going to get. Look at these shoulders.

The owner of the shoulders said that there was in fact a person attached to them; one who had no intention of going to bed with him and who happened to think that George Eliot was vastly over-rated anyway. No, as it happened, she had started off doing English but had fallen out with one of the lecturers and was in exile in the Sociology Department. But she'd be quite happy to spend the rest of the night arguing the artistic perfection of Ms Austen as opposed to Eliot.

I thought of something Nabokov wrote arguing the other case, or rather for Dickens as opposed to fine, minor arts but I wasn't going to prolong this one. You wonder why a body retreats to spoken stories?

Gareth said that she'd be brave to discuss literature with an expert whose promising career had only faltered when he'd written that George was a half-brother of T. S.

The bonfire was sparking. Mahogany or a paler wood with a darker stain was now falling into embers. Faces were glowing. I'd no idea this archivist had such a gregarious side. I whispered it, then. Was there family, here? No but it was going to happen soon. He'd leave a message for me. Best to be in a group, a session, first time.

The Whitehall Road Session got going. Daniel prepared his own bow and took down a case. This one had been given him in Plymouth. But it wasn't Scott Skinner or Greig-Duncan or Shetland style picked-up from any recordings I'd heard. There was a classical hint, still there in the bowing but something else as well. Something more Eastern-European than Scottish Traveller. I wanted to know the other side, hearing that, the family who had reared him. Jewish? Ones who'd fled in time? But then I was off. It's a sort of oblivion when you lose the individual notes and the strings ring. Hell's teeth, someone really could hit the bodhran. It was the exile from the English Department. A lover of Jane Austen. Impossible. But I'd a story to tell.

Another day. Another session. Another group of people with, perhaps, Daniel and me the constant factors.

A very tall man who couldn't be much older than me was sitting on a low stool. His hair was bleached. He said he was kicking himself he hadn't brought his drums along. They were played by the hands, not sticks. Just to contribute something since it looked like everyone else here could sing, play or tell a story.

Daniel and I had come in the van, last to arrive. It was somewhere in the maze of one of the biggest Council schemes. It had taken a bit of finding. One thing was sure, that guy couldn't be one of Daniel's relatives. Had to be either Zimbabwe or South Africa.

The woman of the house was easy to talk to. She hadn't bothered giving her name or getting mine. No, I didn't play anything but I was a good listener. And liked stories. I'd come to the right house. Aye, a friend of Daniel, like.

She kent I'd a story in me too. Funny that way, like.

Then I knew we'd already met. She'd sold me my shoes at the Friday market. Veldtschoens I could keep getting resoled for the rest of my life. Maybe she'd tell me how long I was going to live as well.

I looked across the room and there was Daniel, like me squatting on the floor. He was sitting by a man who cradled a fiddle in his lap and was discussing the instrument. This was quite an old one, German-made.

In a straight-backed chair a very old man was sitting bolt-upright. He'd a neckerchief and a gold chain to his pocket. He'd be ready for off soon. He just bided across the road. She'd walk with him and then they'd have a wee something.

I gave up then, trying to fit together all the bodies in the room, the relationships. Shook hands with the old man before he retired for the night. Spoke then to a guy I'd met before, at some other session. Storyteller, singer and piper – maybe in that order. Tall man.

We both spoke with the big fair guy. The storyteller asked him where the twang was from.

No, not Australia. He'd been raised in South Africa but he'd never call himself South African. Mind you, Australia wasn't that different. Look what they'd done to the Aborigine. But he'd got out, on the move. Was that worse, running away?

This is still a Travellers' hoose, ken, though aebody wis kinda settled here noo. Ye've nae kinda need tae apologise tae anybody here for moving on.

I noticed Daniel was still talking, to a man with a fiddle. He was quieter than I'd seen him before.

No polite refusals now. The South African guy and I gave her a hand to get the tea and pieces. These were for meat-paste and the brown ones for cheese-spread. There you go, boys, a pile each.

Passing them round, I noticed the photo Daniel had got redone from an old print, a new negative made and set in an oak frame. A younger face but still with the watch-chain and waistcoat and a brave cravat. The only travelling he'd do now was to the sideboard when the shelves got dusted.

Then after creepy stories from the woman of the house, alternating with himself's, till late, one old fiddle came to life. Daniel's stayed in its case.

And here was branches in winds. Lanes that led into each other and then could never be found again. A sore thing, being lost where you thought you knew every turning. Some roads changing. Some rights of way gone to disuse. This from a man who'd not been persuaded to a recording studio or folk-club yet. Only thing that could have followed him was Daniel's voice, the one that had just about taken the tin roof clean off the blue van on the Stonehaven road.

Big Daniel lifted up the German fiddle and fingered the strings. He put it back down again. Only then did we become aware of the number of ticking clocks in this room. They'd been subdued behind the earlier sounds. Now they were all in sight and in hearing. I might have expected polished horse-brasses but not these. That old man must have collected most of them. Some were ships' chronometers – these tended to be round. Those rescued from decayed country-houses tended to be square-set.

Then the tall man who still looked sunswept said he didn't much fancy going back to his own cottage. It wasn't that far out of town but it still seemed kind of like other people still lived in it and hadn't given it up to him. He'd have to arrange a big party to fill it with a new atmosphere. He'd get the date to us.

Daniel seemed disorientated. I thought maybe the big clocks reminded him of another big house, one he didn't talk about.

Maybe the problem was that this room was like the end of a quest. He'd told me that quests don't have endings. It was he who had warned me to wander amongst the whins if that was where they led at any one time. Because destinations were dodgy places to aim for, rooms or islands or degrees. No halts, no endings. Only ways you've gone and ways to go.

Compost
Attic
A Length of Rope
Groups

Recipe for life:
flow of liquid through a pipe of constant diameter

$$L_m = \sqrt{\dfrac{Q_m}{D \times d/_D \times F_{pv} \times E \times m + lm + lm + vm}}$$

$\left.\begin{matrix} L_m \\ Q_m \\ D \end{matrix}\right\}$ known $d/_D = required$ Demander capella M

Compost

Calum had a formula. He wrote it out for me often enough. Might still have a copy in a folder somewhere. You could recognise a square-root sign here and there but that's about all. The symbols combined to contain Calum's philosophy but the whole thing was tightened by giving the full lecture to people like me who were beyond redemption. Maths only came alive in navigation. Angles to the horizon or to some astral body you've identified. Discovering distance from the relationship of known items. I could get that.

Calum's formula also had a practical application. The flow of liquid through a pipeline. This was a constant. Once found, the figure was important to a design team. The firm in Sevenoaks had carried out plenty of installations on the strength of it.

His point was this – daft people thought they'd invented a basic law by writing it down. Of course they'd only hit on a latent part of the material world, as created, he said. This was the relationship between art and science and arrogant human beings needed to be aware of it, he said.

At times I thought Calum could have a fair stab at playing the arrogant human being, himself. But you could understand it. Displaced peasant roots in Sutherland to well-heeled high bourgeois Scot, via I don't know how many generations or countries. Gone bust in Kent. Recovering stability in a bungalow, high enough in North Berwick to be aware of the Bass Rock. Stevenson territory with David Balfour trapped on yet another island. Finances then going stable while seeing sons through further education. Then making a new living for himself, the work seeing him into his seventies. Couldn't quite afford to retire, not even up our way.

When he drove me through the town's only roundabout in the A-35 – that's the car not the road – he asked me what I thought of the Swiss-cottage style roof, to our right. I thought he was inviting an argument, ready to say how bloody inappropriate it was for Lewis. I told him I thought it looked like a good use of space and tidier than some I'd seen. I was being tested. This was one of his jobs.

Calum believed that people who could not get science and religion together were damned beyond the time-span of this world. So were younger, irresponsible types who listened to amplified music which would soon reduce the country to anarchy. Unless they were redeemed by an interest in Organic gardening. I've seen him bent over into talk, his own face ploughed by lines. Big discussions with some guy in a pony-tail and sawn-off denims. Distributing leaflets for the Henry Doubleday Soil Association.

Going up the new road to *Greenhill* must have used a good part of a gallon and I wondered how this was accounted for in his ecology. I think he saw that Austin as a late example of car-building before life expectancy was deliberately reduced. Before Unions, plastic trims, the renewed Japanese nation and American dollars had jointly mucked-up British motor-car production. I'd come by for a yarn and see his feet stretched out from under it. The jacket would be off, on a peg in the garage. The bottoms of the overalls – they had creases – moved up high enough to show khaki twill appearing under the blue.

No, I couldn't help him with the car, but if I could just barrow some of that soil into the concrete housing he'd cast for it, drainage built-in. I'd to watch it, though. It was still tender.

I broke it, misjudging the welded hoop around the wheel of the barrow. A tablespoon sized chip of concrete fell to the path. I thought of just placing it back on. Could maybe sneak back up with Araldite when the light was gone. But he must have sensed something because I heard the hiss of the welding torch die. He hauled himself out. Bloody younger generation. The most careless shower. Then I got a puncture in the wheelbarrow tyre. This time I retreated down Stewart Drive before he chased me. But I was to work with him again, more than once.

He was selling the Austin. This came out when I was sitting up front on one of the seats he had covered in tweed. He noticed me glance to the back seats, which he had brought back to life with leather polish. Maybe he knew I was also counting up the the hours he'd spent under the chassis of the thing.

A sort of betrayal. The last of quality construction – or maybe second-last. My father's first car was an A-40 which had done him eleven years, on two engines. Not in it at the same time.

I was trying to lighten things. It's not always best. This time it was OK. He agreed that selling the A-35 was treachery. Not so long ago he'd had the exhaust done. The chap in the pit turns, like a hospital consultant, to his apprentice, and begins a discourse in Gaelic. I gave the man a nudge, Calum says. Asked him if he wouldn't mind speaking in a language I could understand as it was my exhaust system under discussion. No, he said, can't do it. English is too poor a language for that job.

Calum turned the corner with finesse and we went up the road to the house he'd designed for himself and Elaine. Out front, the bonnet and the Austin badge gleamed in the first sun after rain. She was as near the black sedan as I was going to get. Undeniable style.

The hand brake was on. He wasn't in the usual hurry to make a move. The contracts were exchanged.

I remembered the living-room of *Greenhill*. It had a comfortable sort of austerity with a stone fire-place and clean lines. Calum had gathered most of the materials used throughout the house. He'd been proud of the mantelpiece timber. Part of a plank he'd rescued from the builders who were steering wheelbarrows over mud, on it. Supervised all the building but acted as mason on his own hearth. Neither of them had wanted anything ostentatious. They'd had all that before, in Kent and North Berwick. He'd taken the blueprints out from a drawer. So I could see how the physical reality had emerged from the lines.

We'd better head in. The pause had allowed him to roll a cigarette. It was all right. Everything had been arranged with the new owner. These people couldn't care less about the garden.

I had the fork. He carried the sacks. First time I noticed that Calum's full height was only about equal to my own. It was the lean frame and gaunt face. A real map, there. Plenty of contours. Reminded you of photos of W. H. Auden in later life, when he said his own face was like wedding cake left out in the rain. Maybe all that neatness had given the impression of strength.

No, Calum couldn't deny that this seemed a fine upright, courteous, sensible and everything else sort of fellow, this one who'd bought *Greenhill.* But he had no interest in growing things. So much for the notion of a civilised being.

The lawns were gone to rustling grasses. The roses in the front garden looked a bit out of hand to me but to Calum they were finished. Black spot. Hardy again. A bit much. All aspirations to perfection were gone from this garden but there were still a few shoots of green. The fates weren't as large as life, to me. But I'd only been around for a bit over the twenty years.

Along the path to the back garden, to dig out the last of Calum's sacred compost. Our mission was to shift the stuff down to his son's house. Calum and Elaine were camping out there till the sheltered-housing scheme, up at Hazelhead, Aberdeen, was completed. Roddy was, of course, teaching today. Maybe there was something to be said for students after all. At least they were generally idle when you needed them.

It was a fine Friday of early autumn sun. The rough but neat little bird-tables were bare. The vegetable beds, a few paces away, could only just be made out from the undergrowth. They hadn't even bothered picking the loganberries. Would have been a heavy crop, this year. I didn't know if it was the right thing to pick a few, going past.

Deviating from our course.

Feathery green made the carrots recognisable and there were a few needles coming through, to suggest onions underneath. I was nearer the patch so bent over and pulled one carrot. It was firm and good. Sandy loam from its root fell to my shirt. The words were in my mouth, something about at least taking the remaining vegetables home because that guy would never use them. I bit them along with the carrot.

We set to digging and bagging. He had the first go with the fork until he had to pass it on, breathing hard. He didn't say a word but took the bag from me and held its neck open. It wasn't simply that I was providing the physical strength, sweating with youth. He was conscious of everything that had to be done and his own driving energy was running the show.

In one sense it was just plain daft to stay there for one second after we'd got what we'd come for. It was pointless even to discuss digging right to the bottom, taking out the fibrous stuff and packing it round the upright pipe in the next wooden section, to have it all ready for a new season's compost.

To Calum, this plan worked with the necessary rhythm of the year. Decayed matter of weeds and peelings was rotted down but could later be extracted from the wooden frames like sections of honey. But he must have known that the new owners, who couldn't be bothered to cut the grass, wouldn't even notice the existence of the composting system.

He won me over. Another half-hour would do it. It was the same feeling I've had when time is tight and you've shown your face at the procession, taken a turn at carrying. Then you see the bus waiting, wheels on the pavement, off the road, while the hearse is being made ready. You don't know whether you're expected to go to the grave-side. What was expected here, I couldn't say but it was pretty clear what was wanted.

He was carrying me along. All right, so the compost was already in the bags but we had to complete our job. It had to be neat.

I set to scraping and tidying and then stuck the fork right into the ground so I could catch my own breath. Colin had disappeared for a minute but returned from the car with a claw-hammer. There was some amount of gear in that boot.

If I'd gather up the short planks, he'd get nailing. Calum didn't miss one, didn't pause. No great effort, but steady. They all fitted there, slats salvaged from fish-boxes, his composting system. Everything complete and done with dignity.

Then he opened himself without bothering to wait till he could return to normal breathing. I could be excused for thinking it was the convoluted scheme of a crazy old man. Fair description come to think of it. This was to have been the last move but the new house wasn't quite the other end of the earth. Visitor's room was included. That was a hint in case I hadn't got it. Elaine said they'd never gone back anywhere and wouldn't start now. But this was the dry east coast. Should suit them. If you're alive you know when it's time to move and, if you don't, you end up offering damn-all to the place.

Elaine and he weren't going to sit about waiting – and while we were on the subject, I could have his dinner-suit, with the tails. I'd been taken by that. He'd never told me about his brother.

And this did come out of the blue. This from Calum whose stories had always been practised, measured and under control.

Successful man, his brother – in the business world but no time for a family. Retired into a luxury apartment with nothing but designer furniture in it. A hell of a long day to fill. But he still couldn't bring himself up to the provinces to see his relatives, not even for a few days. No point to head for. Only thing was, as he'd said more than once, at least his body could go to medical research. To make himself useful. Calum started moving right then and we went abreast from the garden, carrying the tools.

That brother died on a Friday. They didn't find him till late on Monday. It was too late for him to be of any use.

I felt the tug at the roots of my shoulder. It was Calum, taking the fork from my hand. To stow it in the boot of the Austin.

The pelagic fish are shoaling off reefs, in sea-lochs and in open water. East-Coast pursers are not yet on the scene so now is the time to take herring and mackerel on bare hooks and small white feathers or touches of tinsel. A line-caught herring is a perfect thing that still possesses all its scales. Then there's the brindled back of a mackerel.

At first you can't see past the obvious. A herring split with a thumb along the backbone, dipped in oatmeal and it all browning in its own oil. A mackerel with slit flanks, hours from the sea, brushed with lemon juice, salt and paprika, going golden over charcoal.

But you could try dipping herring in seasoned flour, frying them, before placing them nose to tail, to cool in cider or wine vinegar, black peppercorns, bay-leaves, allspice and juniper berries. Leave for two to three days and eat cold with salad. As to the oven: my mother did potted herring, biting their tales, baked in vinegar and eaten cold.

Don't despair at the mention of raw salt herring. All these barrels we sent all over Europe and none of these fish were ever boiled. First soak the herring in fresh water then fillet and skin it. Cut into strips and place with firm cold potatoes, gherkins and diced apple in a salad. Try a mayonnaise made from blending olive oil and that full-cream Greek yoghurt.

Back to mackerel. There's a German way, baked with slices of sharp apple. Or layered with gooseberries.

Calum's son was renovating a place just up from Bayhead. Not a bad little town-house. Rather a nice bay-window. Room for conversion. In fact that was the point. I could put my talent for destruction to good use. Bring a friend. Everybody welcome. He and Roddy could shovel it all out after. What they needed was someone to swing a sledgehammer.

I did have a friend visiting for a couple of weeks. The air was lighter with another woman in the house. Helen was a medical student but we were both of the destroying generation. I was amazed Calum didn't write out the formula for her as he shook some Gold Blend into the Aviemore pottery cups, the ones with a faint thistle. A man preoccupied.

He issued me with a sledgehammer. A dainty five-pound effort for the lady. A stilson to share. We were given overalls and the three of us went singly up the loft-ladder. Calum pointed to the partitions which had to come down. Some of them were plasterboard but some were the older type of construction: plaster on a strapping of lath. Helen and I had tea-cloths over our mouths and noses. Health and safety, late seventies style. Earlier in the decade you'd have had nothing at all.

We did become possessed as we swung. The walls fell and the dust rose. I opened the skylight, which we'd been told was about to be replaced by a larger Velux and both of us gulped in air. Then we looked. Calum's head also appeared. It was all suddenly very quiet.

Some good wood here. But we were all horrified at how little time the demolition had taken. Yes, you lot are pretty good at pulling things down, he said. I thought of The Who smashing guitars against amps and felt implicated.

Helen knew to dismiss all this as a strange thanks and asked why the low attic was divided further, into stalls. She'd seen a black-house and many houses in Spain where the animal accommodation was close. But this was an attic. It couldn't have been for beasts.

Calum could see it all. The whole plan would have been simple. Tiers of bunks at both ends with a cubby-hole in the middle. You could see where the opening into the chimney had been bricked-up. The shifts would have done their cooking there. One group eating quickly, so as not to lose their sleeping time and the following shift's working time. Then raising the sleepers, the kettle boiled again for them, in return for the warmth in their bunks.

He could decipher the system at a glance. That's what a background in management does for you. The only problem was guessing what would happen from midnight Saturday to midnight Sunday. Unless they were all travelling distance from home. Or half of them, that's all it would take. Or relatives in the town.

Calum asked us to stay and eat. Roddy was working late, again. But we wanted to get the dust off. Returned to my mother's flat. She'd have a big fire on for the hot water.

We took turns to use the shower then went subdued to our fried chops. My mother responded to the vision of the herring-girls. This was where East and West Coast culture met. Maybe even came together via Baltasound, Shetland. In our kitchen, the window would just catch the tops of the pines at the other side of the inner harbour. About the same distance from the pier as the herring-girls, billeted in that attic. The harbour extended further up the head of the bay then. You could see it in the photos.

For Calum, the next part of the equation happened in Aberdeen. He was getting the details organised. Elaine was at their other son's, near Aviemore, until she got the all-clear. Just about there. This was definitely the final flitting. Had he said that before?

He was impressed with the design of the scheme, pointing out details like the trim, preventing ingress of water at the eaves. He'd negotiated a few square feet of ground from the gardener. Expanding only slightly from their allotted slot in the Reservation. But the thing was, it appeared they had a connection with one of their neighbours. Originally from the Island. Garrabost, no Habost was it? One of these Bosts anyway. How it had come up in the conversation, he couldn't remember. She'd worked in the town when she was a girl, but that was only the start of it. Fraserburgh, Peterhead, Yarmouth – she'd been to them all. Taking trains to follow the fishing. And trying to save a few pounds to send home. Some of her pals saving to get married. She said she'd had a good life.

But where in Stornoway? Well, she couldn't say for sure. It was a long time ago. And Bayhead, Keith Street, Kenneth Street, Scotland Street – they were all full of attics like that. In-between the barrel stores. Keith Street could ring a bell. Now she thought of it there was a lot of banter about being so near Al Crae, the undertakers.

Calum was triumphant. For him this was the pleasure of a pattern. Out of the neatness of this link came forth significance. He went to the fridge. Hesitated for a second then also went rummaging in the freezer compartment. He brought out both cream and ice-cream to have with the apple-pie. He'd have to top-up his cholesterol level before Elaine came down. Never get away with this sort of pudding then.

Maybe he was also caught up in the history of it. Great bustle of commerce for the Baltic markets. I could only think of all that silver, all the fortunes made for someone else by these women with the fast knives, before their bodies fell into someone else's sleep. All these hours and them laughing, bantering with it, against a huge drift of ache.

First check your crab.
Black spot or a liquid tone
put it back where it came from
– it takes time to dress one for dinner.

Mrs Beeton shows you how to drive a skewer
at an inward angle through each eye
so you can immerse it with a better conscience
in water previously brought to the boil.

The shell will break along the dotted line.
Keep firm brown meat and waxy orange.
Scrub the shell to serve as a dish.
Remove the gills and split the carapace.
A small pronged tool will help you separate
stringy white flesh from brittle calcium.

Nutcrackers for the claws
strong knife to split legs
and the meat amasses.

The mayonnaise can be lightened with yoghurt,
freshened with flat blades of parsley,
only the youngest shoots of dill.
Lemon added, dribble by drop.

A Length of Rope

The link was a hawser, thick enough to dock a liner. You could have walked along its length. Wouldn't even need a pole to assist your balance. Slack rope walking. Threads of something synthetic were pleated into a squat length of hugeness. It was now partly frayed at the outer strands. Still have most of its strength in the inner cores. I wondered how long the full length had been. Original piece of string question. And did you start with the beginning or the end of a rope? Stories of attempts to tow islands from a great iron ring, wide as a norseman was tall. Set into a cliff at the Butt of Lewis. Every oar on board, bending sea, in the struggle to move the colonised landfall nearer home. Up in Shetland or here in Orkney the Scandinavian links were stronger still.

All colour had bleached from this rope. Wear and oil had given it the natural texture and shade of hemp. But its history could be colourful. Now it was a fender, held in position round the rim of the small pier by rough ties of turquoise and orange. It was pretty effective. The smooth blue resin of the ferry had been cushioned while landing its assorted deliveries and two passengers.

The vessel then took-on large squat boxes with thin rope handles. These had bore holes. Black-green seaweed dripped from them. The cargo which really justified the ferry's detour up yet another tide rip to yet another island. Lobsters to catch the flight from Kirkwall.

Prices were falling fast. Something about imports from Canada. Maybe caught by the descendants of so many Islanders who'd become more Scots than Norwegian. And now Canadians. The sons of those who had sailed in the emigrant ships, as late as the 1920s. Some, still later, if they thought they had skills or strengths to sell.

No-one knew how far down the price could slump. He was glad it wasn't his way of making a living. He only got on the ferry when he had to, for supplies. He left the real seagoing to his son. The boy had never wanted to be anywhere that wasn't wet. That's how the big rope-fender and a lot more besides, had appeared. It was a present salvaged from the waste of a tanker or rig. Maybe a supply-boat, high at the bow and a long low hull for handling anchors and tows. These things were getting too big, altogether. But his son didn't see it like that. He was at Flotta.

You'd think this hefty wee guy must have got his healthy beaten face from years as a boatman. But no, he was a farmer. Didn't mind thon blue stuff, just to look at. The inter-island crossing was long enough for him. But his boy took pleasure as well as his career from the sea. Sail or engines. Never really took an interest in the land. Except that he was good at tractor-engines and gearboxes. He'd usually get stuck-in there when he was back, which was quite a lot now, thanks to Flotta and the North Sea. Last time he'd been home, he'd set to maintaining the pier. Was that land or sea now, or neutral territory. Eh, which?

This man in the deep blue overalls, his good ones for the visit to the Mainland, said he was coming home from a day in the town and a night at his sister's there. A day squandered between the crossing, the bus and the bank. He got most else here or from the catalogue. See the supplies coming in. We turned to watch. Two nylon nets, one full of cabbages, the other with oranges, were being picked up by the merchant now, after being thrown up to the jetty, from the ferry.

That'll soften them a bit. Just as well, for my teeth. Too far to go to the dentist. So how long have you got here, anyway? Wait a minute now, there was the rest of the morning and the full afternoon before the ferry would be back. Well, I could make it to to the north end, I looked fit enough for that. And I'd the boots for it.

Now, if I was going out there, I'd pass some stones that were worth seeing. Aye and come to think of it, I might see the other end of that big rope. He'd given that to the people up the north end, though he didn't know what use they had for it. No pier, there. I'd get a lift as far as the tarmac strip went, by his own house as it happened. So I'd see where I'd to come for my cup of tea on the way back.

He had to be kidding but he wasn't. No MOTs here. We jumped onto a chassis with an engine, gearbox and seat. It did have four wheels too but not much else. It did have a dashboard but no glass above it. Even the primer was gone so you couldn't guess what colour it had been. One light spilled its bulb down on a wire. No number plates. A chrome badge to say it was a GT something.

Get in it or on it, whatever you like. Anything went here if it could go, if I saw what he meant. Plenty of warning before any vehicle inspectors came looking for paperwork. This car had come to him after a crash on one of the other islands. He'd bid more than the scrappie and had it ferried for free. Contacts again. Here it was. Nowhere here takes long to get to. The north end was a bit of a plod for him but I'd have no bother with the track.

I followed one fence but then saw the shore and swerved to go that way. Walking on pebbles, giving way to sand. Bones of driftwood on all ridges. Bottles in colours that didn't fit into any cycle of shore, sea or sand life. All loud with a variety of birds. I was happy just to note their variations. Didn't need to recognise the species.

Things slowed. I couldn't guess how long it took to reach the tip of the island with its one long low house. There was a tall figure and several small ones in the garden. She seemed to be the mother, in well-worn jeans made into shorts. The children were trying to gather the weeds she'd picked out. Stuff going everywhere. Signs of the wee ones being fed up. Work stopped. You couldn't just pass by unnoticed.

No, I was just here for the day. No I didn't know anyone else on the island. Only the man I'd met on the way over. A farmer – his son was at sea.

Her man was at sea today, out for crabs and mackerel. Just a small boat. He'd be back by tonight. She was ready for a break. The kids didn't see many people, outside of school. They might want to show me things and pull me about. I couldn't get out of that.

She'd seemed more shy than the farmer but here was me following her, dipping under a low lintel. If it was more difficult for her to have company, did that make her offer of tea mean more? The children were squeezing in. I wasn't sure how many there were.

My ear was pulled. I was steered back out to a castle of fish-boxes then a tunnel, shored-up with the same bleached slats. Through the arch of a whale-bone, probably a jaw, while smoke began to rise from the house to the warm air. Live geese and salads were separated by fish-nets. The bell of a cow or goat sounded from somewhere. A wooden wheel hung still at the top of a tower which was also a collage. The child who seemed eldest was deep-brown. Must have a Middle East parent. Maybe part-Asian. He told me the wheel ran their television when the wind blew.

We were all back in to eat something. The older ones were at school. No they didn't try to do everything alone. You couldn't, even if you wanted to, but Bill and she did quite a bit. Veg and stuff was expensive and not that good. But if the boat had come today the van would be round.

Others had lived there. It was very free, some good times. But it hadn't worked out. Somebody repaired all these roofing slabs. Someone else rigged up that miniature set, run off the batteries from the wind generator. Did that seem a kind of contradiction? Maybe it was but she couldn't keep this lot amused and do the garden and prepare food all the time. Look it was easiest if I just helped myself. There was plenty of crab – no real market for it now but it was just as good as lobster when you got into the shell. Any amount of salad. Had I tried endive?

She and Bill gathered seaweed a lot. No, they knew there was edible kinds but that was something they hadn't tried, yet. Just the usual kind to rot down for fertiliser. That's what everybody else had used when they grew food, here. Some people still had potatoes. Most of the other crops, any grain, was for the animals. They had some calves, sheep, two goats. I had to try the sausage if I didn't mind big lumps of garlic. And that was dried intestine, not plastic, round it. She cut some from where it hung, above the wood stove and sliced it, red and pink-white inside the salt encrusted skin. It and the sourdough bread, the crab and salad, were good. I was hungry after the walk but this must be their store. Provisions built-up in a time of comparative plenty.

Look, I wasn't to piss about with dishes or anything like that. She had some coffee somewhere. She'd make some if I just played a bit. That was the most useful thing. That would be best.

And then they were over me in a blur of names and nips, looking for attention. We ran. They steered me to another shed with the irregularities of driftwood in its make. Bill made all these toys. He was in the boat today. They weren't allowed out there with him. They had dodgems. It was all right. He let them bump as much as they liked.

They were protected by a fender of thick, plaited rope, cut to fit around each one. We played some more. Did some hide and seek. Slowed down. They showed me some of their treasures, brought from individual boxes back inside.

I was welcome to stay but if I had to go, I'd meet Bill another time. He liked talking to different people. The quickest way was back over the fields, rather than following the shore again.

No, no it was OK, I'd get some tea or something back in his house – I didn't even know his name. Then get the ferry.

Wait a minute, she had some cheese I could bring. No, maybe not. Some of the local people were funny about goats' milk. Maybe not bother now. Leave it another day.

Her voice went with me the shorter route to the farmer's door. He had a pot of tea stewing. I told him while I remembered, the rest of his son's rope was fendering toy trucks. He liked that. How many children? So one last couple brought them all up, all the kids left there, after the rest of the commune chased off to India or God knows where?

I didn't know. Just that there was a lot of children and others at school. She was doing a great job.

She was. She had staying-power that one. The fellow she was with now, too. Bit chancy on the sea though in that old boat. Maybe it was unfair, what most folks said. Maybe most folks were unfair, full bloody stop. But you got frightened by stuff that was out of the ordinary. He'd gone a bit that way, himself. You can understand it though. You're an Islander yourself. People like that can be a threat, buying up the crofts and only playing at farmers. The ones with a bit more money are the dangerous ones. Ones that sold a place somewhere else where prices were higher and could outbid local folks. Nobody here wanted that place at the north end. So that was different, like. Good luck to them.

Old families went. New ones didn't usually stay that long. But that woman had stuck to it, up there beside that bloody windmill or whatever the hell it was. Mind you people sold-up by choice. No-one was starving though no-one was making real money either. Maybe you couldn't cope with it these days, not being close in touch. Everyone keeping more to their own patch, so the island seemed more isolated.

We sat at a deal table. I asked about the fiddle on the nail. He said he only scraped at it once a month or so, the fiddle that was, not the nail.

Only when he was alone. He hadn't what it took to play in company. As for all these books in the house, they'd always been there. He didn't look them out much and didn't add to the piles. The son wasn't a bad reader.

Wait now, though, I wouldn't miss the boat. He'd something to tell, wouldn't take a minute. Could tell it to me because I'd be away soon. He couldn't write-off all these people who'd passed through and made their mark at the north end, not out of hand, like. I could see he was alone now, except when the boy was back. He wasn't a widower, no, not exactly. Not legally, anyway. Dora, she'd been called and it was during the war, down south. He spent a lot of his war in these training camps. She was like you'd see in an old photo album, but he didn't have a picture left. She was a girl in a tight hat and a long skirt, standing with one hand on a bicycle. Him stationed down near her, like.

It was more common then, things going wrong in childbirth. She hadn't come through it. But a son was a son whether or not your name was on some bit of paper. His own mother had been the one to swing it. It had taken a fair bit of doing. Dora's mother had been dead against it, dead against him for a start and then their grandson living the other end of the earth to them. These folk don't know where Orkney is. Somewhere near Iceland if you ask them.

Everyone up here thought they'd all gone crazy but his mother had gone down with him. Met everybody face to face. Stood with him. She'd learned to be strong when his own father didn't come back from the sea after the First War. They'd done all the papers, had to do the legal adoption. But his mother didn't mind saying this was his natural son.

Things had worked out not bad. Except for the land. The boy lived for the sea. Mind you he could always sell the farm and put it towards the boy's own boat. Still hurt, that thought did. He was coming round to it. You'd to come round to a few things if you lived long enough. I'd think

I was sure of my ideas now. No compromises at my age. Aye, he knew the boy was his own man already. He'd sell this ground sometime. That'd be his own affair. So long as he just came and went now as he wanted. Nothing strained.

He drove me to the ferry. The car survived the trip. So did we. We got out and after a bit my fingers relaxed from holding on to whatever bit of metal might stay attached. I noticed he was now in an older set of overalls. The face over them was as seamanlike as ever.

He said it again, how it was good there was some life back up at the north end. He'd be over there yet one of these days. Have to be by foot. Pity the road just stopped where it did.

Grez Sur Loing soup

Talk art with a Finnish painter, Swedish sculptor, till late.
Jointly decide that if you're cooking fish for everybody
and it's impractical to go to the Hebrides and catch them,
you should take the artists' dinghy upstream
between islands and against the flow to
the town of Nemours, favoured by Louis.

So you meet for breakfast and row for it.
Portage between willows.
To arrive at the time of the lunch-break.
So it's late when three return downstream
laden with hake and every breed of head from the shop
because you said you'd also make a soup.
Many lemons and a bunch of parsley.
Well-travelled mussels.
Heavens open. Colleagues know to provide
a modicum of whisky, if they're to eat tonight.

The stock pot is macabre. I add to it with
one perfect bream, caught on worm from a willow
as a token from the Loing. Any poison will dilute.
Now strain and make intense with finely chopped onion,
bay and garlic, deep tomato, dry white wine.
Reduce down as you would a poem.
Mussels and herbs when all are seated.

Hake steaks can look after themselves in the oven.
On fennel and leeks, softening in butter.

Griddle-bread made rich with milk,
stirred into flour crumbled with butter
and eggs since, it's an occasion.

One of the group said another's approach was religious, mine was narrative. Later, when all these fish began to swim from my words, he asked if they were religious fish or sexual fish. Another, basically the tutor-come-producer, asked if you could write yourself into situations. Yet another asked how you got emotion into words. No short-age of questions.

All trailing ends. All people excited with each other. Two in the group falling and staying in love and making children. One gaining the first Student Rectorship. Losing his wife to cancer. One taking early retirement to be a consultant on ecological matters, documenting trace elements. Dying before his poems were collected.

One gaining the grades and becoming eminent in her field. First, the assistant editorships. Then the editions appearing – *Women In Scottish Fiction*. An invitation to a wedding or two. News of more than one divorce, filtering through.

One sharp dresser, white cigarette for emphasis. Her own bylines from quite early on. And a more casual dresser then, a power-dresser now: a realist with good memories. Gave up creative writing a long time ago. Good on reports. The two medical students. The unpredictable one became a psychiatrist. The one fluent in Spanish helped me at a demolition once. I don't know what she's doing now but she isn't a doctor.

One, floating back in her writing to a box-bed in a tenement. Between that and girdle scones in stone houses. The clarsach, the piano, the balanced distribution of creativity. And yet an element, something near jealousy, at those who drive at one art in an obsessive way.

Some good work done by all. Warm people making a few mistakes. The tall Black-Isler who told the story of a slow journey to India and a faster flight home when sick. He came to love a philosopher who never wrote any more of her tight, observed, amoral and effortless poems. She only wrote when she had a need to. But the few other moves towards couplings were illusory. Mine certainly were. Maybe that's what was meant by the question of writing yourself into situations.

Don and I had a correspondence. The blue airmails went back and fore for a while after he had to return to the States and our group lost its song-writer. Hint of the other yank also called Don, the Maclean guy. I took to our Don when he sang his song about soldiers on decks somewhere and then was blasted by flames thrown from the one who'd been in the Marines. Yet the former soldier later arranged the sponsorship for Don's return for the Fringe show. Free speech and no grudges.

I thought of Don's song when the Falklands Crisis was fully wound-up, mood and melody just staying with me for days. The headlines appeared while I was doing a later variation of that type of show, with musician friends often outnumbering the audience in a draughty Edinburgh hall – the Folk Festival in the spring of that year. Then, in the Autumn, doing something similar in Aberdeen and being shown the privately printed, gilt-embossed covers of a celebratory edition produced by a former Marine. That former Marine. Turned businessman, then student then first Student Rector. Honour returned to Britain via the South Atlantic.

But I'd had another correspondence in blue envelopes stamped Goose Green. From a guy called Scott, an individual, yes, but, in relation to me, one from another group; other circle. He'd gone to be a gaucho in a poncho. He'd ridden into Steinbeck territory. The Company owned everything. You fell out over conditions and you didn't get meat. Couldn't buy oranges for your kids, in the store. He'd got out, not long before the Argentinians went in.

My correspondence with Don concerned duck-eggs. I said he'd been right. The last few days in the UK (he didn't know then that this deal had been arranged for the Festival) were for a wild trip. A friend was also going back to the States. They were hiring the car in the afternoon so they'd come out from Aberdeen. We walked the cliff line to Dunnotar. The battlements grassed over. I was getting used to the idea of always a rig somewhere on the skyline. A lot of your guys out there, folks.

I was pointing out the nest, just at the edge, to his friend. Maybe there was that bit of showing her the hard-edged islander, as I put out a hand to take one of the four eggs. Don said, if my scent was on the others they'd get abandoned.

Then we had a cup of tea at Stonie and they left to get an hour's sleep before heading North. Next day was the big push. John o' Groats to Lands' End. Why not? After they'd gone I went to make the big omelette. It was too late, too warm. When I cracked the shell there was blood and black in the yolk. That's what was in the first airmail. Had to tell him.

Pity I wasn't able to be as direct, face to face, when we all met up in Edinburgh. We were room-mates in that bustling flat and one night I didn't come back. Neither did the one who performed, each day, that one poem in Scots though she looked Pre-Raphaelite under the lights. He was called Billy, the man in her poem, and he was gallus.

As you do, so many days out from your routines, amongst company, I drifted. It was the year of the big Degas show. We went together. Then we gravitated down Dundas Street, to see her friend who lived below street level. Down the railings, past lace-work at a window and here we were. Her friend had also been to the big exhibition. I'd been amazed at the sculptures, how big the effect for their modest size. And we were talking Degas. The nature of intimacy. In pastels or in bronze. Enough detail to catch a temporary position for keeps. And a woman's arms holding her own hair, when washing, made as strong a form as another, in a ballet movement.

There was no need for us to go back. I could have the couch here and the girls, both with their long hair, went to sort something next door. I had to listen to know when the bathroom was free. I lay awake long after the water ran away from each of them, brushing their teeth, in that small space between our two rooms.

Next day we did the lunchtime show and went to eat something, still the two of us drifting together. We went to the Student's Union, where the Festival Times appeared first. The Review might be today. They had come back for some photographs and everything.

It was a good review. I realised I was hungry and we went to the counter. A hot plate and then the salad bar. I wanted hot food but found myself pointing to this and that just because it was on display. Then walked to a table with a plate of salads. She joined me.

Salad places were great in Edinburgh but this was prepared stuff, bought in bulk and preserved in bitter vinaigrette. My empty stomach didn't like this treatment. I didn't get tight like this before performing but this must be what they called nerves. And then I was talking and the words saying that I had to tell her ...

She stopped me before it got too silly. Spoke fast. This kept happening to her. She liked being friends. Too much on top of her this year to think of relationships, anything like that. Just wanted to be among friends.

Couldn't stay there with her, afterwards, and found the door without knocking down any chairs. Looking for a whiff of the East-coast air amongst the diesel. Shit, sleep was what I needed.

No-one in the flat except a subdued Don. He'd come back on a high, flown in to do the week's run but also hoping to build something with ... Yep, somebody staying in this very flat. Well, she wasn't here now. Where had we all got to?

... *this keeps happening to me* ... was what she said.

It takes ten years to write a clear poem. Olaf Hauge, the Norwegian put it something like that. I reckon a story takes fifteen, sixteen, just to see it. There are a few poems and stories which write themselves but they've been waiting to come out.

Don and I both fell in love but only apparently with the same woman. We all fell in love with each other that week. It doesn't happen often enough to let you get used to it, to think you understand it. So maybe you adjust your eyes, trying to focus on one particular person.

Maybe things people did, then or later, bug you. No doubt I bug plenty of the others in the team. People may feel they've made mistakes and ask themselves how they wrote themselves into a situation. But something stays.

This week, in an old hotel that's refurbished into studios but is a refuge of bantering ghosts, all the residents fell in love. Another group. Painters, sculptors, writers. Acrylics, resins and Toshiba laptops. We went walking where Corot and Sisley went painting and drifted back to gather items of food from our individual galleys. We prepared the communal meal in sight of the river where Stevenson secured his canoe to an iron bolt in our garden.

First, I knew only an excitement of nerves, needing to put something in the stomach. Then, as we all couldn't help looking intently at each other, curious and a bit naive, it became clear what was happening.

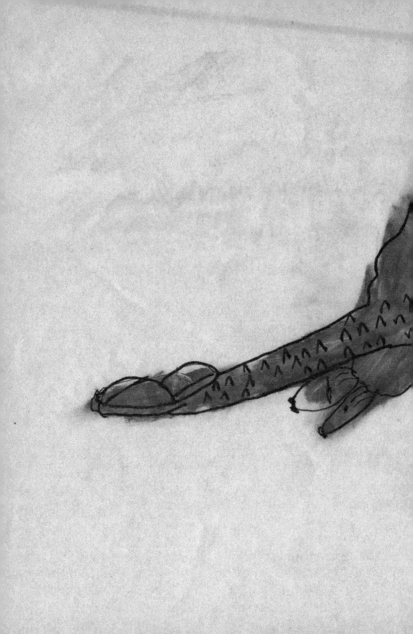

Cul de Sac
New Morn
Cyanus
Che Guevara

Catch the brambles when they start to soften.
Look up to Lady Matheson's monument.
First she became Venus de Milofied.
Laudanum would have been merciful.
She was assisted, quietly, out of the Grounds.
Leaving a canopy of decorative marble.
in honour of swollen prosperity:
Matheson-Jardine, floated on poppy-heads.

Add rowan-jelly to the warming fruit.
Crab-apples, demerara, glass of Trawler rum.
Grated cassia. Scraping of nutmeg.
Knob of butter, then the crumble:
butter rubbed into oats and muesli,
the blackest muscavado you can buy.

You can't go wrong with a moderate oven.
Have ready the Mackie's so it will remind you
of vanilla Cabrelli's from similar tubs.

Cul de Sac

It was the place I grew up in. I had to remember that when I last revisited the cul-de-sac. This was during my driving-test and I'd been asked to go past it and reverse back into it. There wasn't any sign of football going on, in the street, at the time. That was strange.

With the seat-belt off and my body twisted round I could get a proper view out the rear window. The fences had never been replaced. Composed of thin slats linked by twists of wire to separate the gardens from the pavements. You could usually widen the gaps by twisting the wire, to make short-cuts. Handy, if the ball went into someone's garden.

Other street-games had revolved around the lamp-post at the far end, where the road ended in a wide T. Back at the entrance into the cul-de-sac there still wasn't any warning sign of the dead-end. Should have been a stubby red road on a longer blue one, all encased within a red triangle. It was easy to get in and out of, except when you'd been asked to reverse that way.

Many, including my own family, had got out. Some, like us, had eventually returned to the same town, if not to the street. Would have, if we could.

Others stayed away. There was a visionary who vanished without trace. Her energy had attracted me into calling for her daughter who was in my class at school. I was usually offered another bowl of mutton broth and a sermon for the way. That was from the mother, not the daughter. She was some speaker but she didn't have to be, with an eloquent head of red hair, worn long but not tied up the way many Presbyterian women did. Evening gatherings took place. The tail of our cul-de-sac was shaken with the volume of unaccompanied psalms. She couldn't last in our street. I don't know where she went. The husband and a grandmother brought up the two daughters.

Some never moved away. One of my near contemporaries delivered meat for a butcher until he died young and sudden and unexplained. His father had been on *The Girl Norma*. About forty foot, black carvel hull, canoe stern. You could get a fry of fish just for the asking.

Another guy still delivers the mails. Now from a van though they've gone back to bikes, round the centre of town. He seems a happy person, operating within a given radius of his home ground. His father was an angler who showed me all these tins of flies, with peacock herl and grouse hackles, tied into lures for trout.

Our cul-de-sac produced one television star but only for a one-off appearance. She was a natural. She had always been a safe neighbour but had a faraway memory of a much shorter street – the only one on her own native Island – Hirta, St Kilda. She returned there with others who'd been evacuated, at the fiftieth anniversary. She remembered which end of Number Three had held the fire and which the bunk-beds the children slept in. Her mother had built up a good fire, smoored it to stay, glowing under the damp dust as long as possible. Given the room a last sweep. Her son became a TV engineer, installing systems that linked to a distant aerial that at last let anyone in the town area receive signals come from the mainland.

Back in our cul-de-sac, a lean boy hadn't been expected to survive a fall from a roof. A summer job. He became a champion cross-country runner, in the army. The most promising footballer we produced got sidetracked. He eventually stopped running from kitchen-job to kitchen, in city after city. Ran away to sea. Down in the galleys, working out of Leith. Used to be deep-sea. Now it's the North Sea: three weeks on, three off. A slight man, for a chef. All that tasting, little and often.

We had an artist. He won his way through the sections for different age-groups, in national competitions. Our cul-de-sac followed the results, seeing them in print, passing the newspaper around at meal times. Once, one of his paintings appeared on the black and white of a tea-time programme. We'd been shouted in from the games that used numbers and arrows written on the kerbs in blue chalk. Always in the same area of the T, probably a central meeting ground, or maybe just a habit.

Our next-door neighbour, who was a joiner, had one of these paintings in his living room. He had bought it or traded it for work or wood. The artist went on through college and had exhibitions in various Arts-centres. I never saw any of them. My family had moved away by then so we were naturally a bit out of touch. There's no new work to catch up with now. He never looked weak or ill. I remember him as a big, broad man with a thick beard.

We also produced a scientist. No doubt he had to work for his eminent position but everyone knew he was going to achieve his research fellowship at Oxford. He looks robust enough now, though he wasn't so fit when he was young. He returns only in the winter, bringing an ice-axe and crampons home. He made the mistake of just letting it slip to his mother that people working on the effect of radiation on cancers couldn't seriously expect to live long past sixty.

Two daughters from the same house both survived in an area of Italy that was almost totally destroyed in an earthquake.

We had two businessmen. They stemmed from the extremities of one side of the central street, going up to the crossbar of the T. First one rose, by making and distributing lemonade. The factory was walking distance, down among the builders' yards, and the bottles were all different colours, a lot of flavours. That business crashed but he was on the go soon enough, with a sweetie-shop, off a close.

The other had a half-share in a pub in Aberdeen which sounds like wet gold. But he got caught between the booms. If he'd been able to hold out another year he'd have made his fortune. I saw him in London, not long ago, managing a Railwayman's Club near Kings Cross. Everything normal prices as opposed to London prices. A lot of Islanders there, Caribbean and Hebridean. But he's had enough of London. Big changes coming to the railways and he was trying to keep ahead of it this time. No, he couldn't go back. It seemed to work out OK for me. Not for him. If you were any sort of different orientation you needed a bigger place. Another city. Had to be.

It occurs to me now that you may think this spectrum is a fake light, too broad for the perimeters of that T shape. Or that I'm seeing the street in an imaginary or heightened way, despite failing my driving test in it. I can't judge how typical it is but these individuals and that street are real. Some of these people lived under the same roof. I haven't classified them, door to door, in family groupings. It might be worth noting that the artist and the scientist were brothers and the woman from St Kilda and the cross-country runner are mother and son.

These are all certainties but the cul-de-sac has also produced possibilities. It may have reared two writers. If you're reading this you can judge one for yourself. What's happened after the red pen has smudged over the pencil marks and the typewriter has had its turn. The other potential writer came out into the open at the Bridge-Club dinner. I sat opposite her and was forced into honesty when she asked what I was doing with myself these days, not putting the degree to use. It was difficult, seated there in the turquoise shadow of the hotel's new curtains, to admit that my only ambition was to write well. I must have looked far from Bohemian, in the suit and tie, so as not to disgrace my mother. A dinner is a dinner.

A silence after my statement was very short and concerned only us. The rest of the table was involved, all in sections of conversations.

She talked first of what her surviving son was doing and what his life-expectancy was and then cut across her own tack to tell me she had filled several exercise books with some memories and thought of going back sometime to see if they made any sense. It was a question of finding enough space around you, wasn't it?

Yes and getting habits of work to meet the need to do it.

Maybe her office-work took up more time than she could afford but she needed to get out among people. She couldn't stay in the house all the time.

Yes, sometimes the space between the walls of your room seemed to shrink. You put shelves up, trying to give a feeling of height and carry the books which had become part of you. You reared a large dog which needed walking and reminded you to get out of that room. I'd had several changes of address since leaving the cul-de-sac but it didn't seem possible to achieve such balanced proximity to your neighbours.

The waitresses were coming round again to take our main-course plates away. Mine was empty so I must have been eating as we were talking. Hers was not. We talked on. When it came to the sweet-course, which was the clinching one, she passed her unfinished pudding across the table to me. I was able to get to the bottom of that bowl.

Make sure you're on watch with the world razor fishing champion,
a master mariner who goes to the shore with his wits and a poke.
Spades are taboo and trowels are frowned upon.
He warns everyone to leave space for a late feed.
Then you really want a five-hour mission with a happy ending
so everyone's starving and Duncan goes below.

He pours the kettle over the animals
while the butter is browning.
Severs sac, and foot. Pats the rest dry.
Steers them round the pan and serves at once.

Or Martin's breakaway forward's dummy:
"See all this, the breadcrumbs lightly fried in garlic,
the good olive oil, the pepper, the wine,
the skillet smoking – now
run a sharp knife down the razor,
a squeeze of lemon on the edible bits.
See, the oil, the pepper, the skillet –
forget all that stuff and just swallow one."

Last Outpost coastguarding happened in a creosoted shed. This was fixed to Holm Point by a Spanish windlass of galvanised wire. Individual items of equipment were controlled from each desk. So you had to physically move from one end of the building to the other, if, for example, you were speaking on the VHF site remoted to Rodel Aerial and then a call came through on the big-set which had the aerial outside.

That MF set had a receiver, enamelled green. It was a Sailor and we all had faith in it since we'd spoken, clear two-way, with St Johns' Coastguard Radio. Once I saw it move across the desk. It was eerie. It was also the night I got taught the higher reaches of the Beaufort scale by what was happening to our building. One more point and it would have been Force 13 – Stornoway Coastguard puts out a Mayday, no, not a relay, just a Mayday. The shack in the sea.

The Watch Officer and I looked at each other. I was sent to investigate. A cow across the fence had got tangled up in the wiring to the aerial. When she moved, the radio moved.

A telex came through and you had to keep the tape in case you needed another copy or had to relay the message. It was easy to put the wrong tape back through. Or ditch it before you read the line that said to send it to somebody else. So you had to hunt through every bloody tape in the wastebasket. This telex said to hoist South cone. That was the black canvas shape to show on our mast as a gale warning. Ivor said to get out and hoist the bloody cone, bloody point downwards. I'd never be a Communicator as long as my arse pointed downwards.

I wasn't going out in that, to hoist a black signal that no-one was going to see in the night. It was blowing a bloody severe gale.

He knew it was blowing a bloody severe gale that's why he wanted me to get out there and hoist the bloody cone. I put up the signal, clinging to the clip so I wouldn't lose the halyard. He'd have me climb the damn pole if I did. Should have been on a windjammer, that man.

Strange thing was, the yarns were something else. Routine done. Best one I heard though, came on the big-set. 2182 Kilohertz, that's International calling and distress.

Wick Radio, Wick Radio, aye-aye, Wick, Wick Radio, are you listening on this one, are you on here, listening this frequency? Over.

Station calling Wick, yes Old Man, have you on this one. What's your vessel's name? Over.

Aye, Wick, thanks for coming back, like, aye, Wick it's the *New Morn* here, that's the Buckie fishing vessel *New Morn*, the *New Morn* here. Over.

Yes, *New Morn*, this is Wick, for a telephone call listen for me channel Yankee. You listen for me 1844 Kilohertz. Over.

Aye, it's the *New Morn*, the *New Morn* here. I got that fine, like, got you fine, but I think maybe we'd better just hing about here, maybe just stay on this frequency? Over.

New Morn, Wick Radio, no, no, Old Man, can't stay on this one, 2182 is a distress frequency. Can't work you on this one. Can't ... Unless you've got a problem, skipper. Everything OK with you? Over.

Aye, it's the *New Morn*, still with you here, aye, aye. Aye, Wick you could say we've a bitty o a problem here. Aye, a bitty o a one, like. She's takin that bitty o water like. Over.

New Morn, Wick Radio, yes I understand your vessel is taking water. What's your position, your position? Over.

Aye Wick, aye, I widna be far oot if I said we'd be three to three-point-five miles affy the Cape, like. Just to the Noreast like, wee touch east o north. That'd aboot do it like. That'd be us. Did you get that? Over.

Yes, *New Morn*, yes skipper, I have you as three-point-five miles nornoreast Cape Wrath. Can you confirm that with a Decca, Old Man, you couldn't give us a Decca reading for that position? Over.

No, Wick, no, I couldna get richt to the Decca richt noo. Hands a wee bit foo here, but that position should do you like over?

Yes, Wick here, got that and how many persons on board? Over.

That's the three loons an mysel like. Jist the fower o us here. The fower o us? Over.

Wick Radio, that's received skipper and what kind of assistance do you require Old Man, what kind of assistance? Over.

Aye, got that Wick, got that like but I widna try an tell ye yer job like. Widna try to do that but I'd say we're beyond the towing stage here. She is takin a fair bit noo like, this vessel, aye, she's takin a fair bitty like. Over.

Yes, skipper. Roger. Sounds like we could do with helicopter and Lifeboat assistance. Concur with that? Over.

Aye, Wick, widna dae any herm, that, aye, maybe better get that yellow one oot here. Widna dae any harm like.

Yes, skipper, Wick here, my colleague is on that now, he's on to the Coastguard now. Should be with you soon. Just one more thing, the present weather, what's the weather and sea conditions with you now? Over.

Aye, Wick, no that bonny a mornin oot here like. No that bonny a mornin tae ask anyone tae come oot tae us like. But we could dae wi a hand noo. That's the loons getting the liferaft ready noo? Over.

This is Wick, then you intend to abandon, confirm you intend to abandon to the liferaft, then this is a distress, this is a Mayday situation? Over.

Aye, it's the *New Morn*, ye can cry it fit ye like but sorry I canna hing aboot tae talk tae ye much longer noo. No that's me. Hiv tae sign-off here, gone me, like.

Mayday, *New Morn*, Mayday *New Morn*, this is Wick Radio, Wick Radio. Over.

Mayday *New Morn*, Mayday *New Morn*, Mayday *New Morn*. Over.

I've heard that silence a few times over the years. Not a good moment. All the action is under way. Telex going with positions. Distress relays. Lot of teamwork happening. This one was just over the five-degree line into Pentland Coastguard's patch, worked from Kirkwall. They had it all in hand. The yellow one from Lossiemouth airborne. Stromness lifeboat launched.

That night, the chopper found these four guys, waiting there in the liferaft, drifting fast. Doesn't always go that way. But that's the way it came on the big-set that night. Heard another ending to the story though. There's a certain radio-operator used to be with Wick Radio, who's down Aberdeen way, when it all gets rationalised at Stonehaven Radio. He's off watch, having a pint when a large whisky arrives in front of him. Wee wiry guy joins him.

Dye mind a nicht, no a very nice one, you sent a yellow paraffin budgie oot Cape Wrath way tae the crew o the *New Morn*?

Communications established. Then said he'd a wee suggestion, like.

Yes skipper, we're always keen to get feedback. I'll make sure all your comments are passed on.

Aye, well ye did a fine job for me that night. Quite pleased to hear that bloody great din above us, I was. The lads as well. That beastie was a welcome sicht, aye. No, it's more a wee suggestion for the folk who agree they Board o Trade Standards like. The Department standards, for the lifejaickets, like.

Well, yes skipper, I'm sure I could pass that on as well.

Just a bit somethin they could dae wi. A wee improvement, like. I mean ye could be doon there, waitin aboot for help, long enough, like. Could be sittin there a fair wee while. Fit ye could be dain wi is jist a wee pocket, like. Jist a wee pocket sewn on, easy tae get tae. Wid jist aboot tak yer smokes an yer matches.

Take any sort of but. Of a cold-blooded nature.
A small halibut is about as good as turbot.
Withdraw it from the market – for the few quid extra
you're going to get, in comparison,
with the profit your wholesaler will score
you're better to eat it or give it away.

Cut into steaks, wash and trim.
Heat the oven and butter the dish.
Melt the butter to sweat the shallots.
Place on the fish and blanket with cream.
Cut with capers, squeeze of lemon.
Black dust of pepper, so from above
you're looking down on the landscape of Iceland.
Serve when it's bubbling.

Cyanus

I hadn't seen the forecast, after the news. The first indication of the blow was when the rowan, just passing the level of the top of the kitchen window, bent right over. Then you could hear the bin lids go. See the bags trapped against the fences.

Next the power went. My mother had done her mad stoker act with the fire. She doesn't know about neutral. Full-ahead or full-astern. Without the juice to keep the water pumping to the radiators, this could get out of hand. I went to the door and darted out to pull the turfs I'd just got settled in. Back inside with them, trying to get the door shut behind me without dropping all the muck. Damp soil made the fire sober.

The tank was boiling already. I put some cold in then ran-off some of the boiling hot. Anyone want a Turkish Bath? But I'd better get the torch and have a look at the tank. You could still hear it rumbling.

Through the trapdoor and up into the belly of the roof. It was like walking along the ribs of a carvel-built vessel. Except that the shape was going the other way. These new houses didn't look much from the outside but they certainly hadn't scrimped on the timber. That roof could carry any weight of planking or tiles. Reassuring. The overflow pipe seemed to be working. The lagged tank was quietening down to a simmer. Good. Couldn't be an airlock.

I realised, that night, we hadn't really moved so far from the sea. I missed the flat up above the harbour. My mother had been allocated this house, in the new scheme, the landward side of town. You still looked to the Approaches to Stornoway, from the front garden. Out to Broad Bay if you turned your head.

The power came back and the worst of the squall seemed to have gone through with the weather-front. I removed the turfs, put them hopefully where they'd come from. My mother resurrected the fire.

Take it easy, now, it might be off again soon enough. I'm just away across the Court.

I crossed the trodden dockens. There were always fankles of blue polypropylene and fluorescent pink buoys around certain houses in our scheme. Creels to fix when you couldn't get to sea. The days when you had to fill in the funny forms for the self-employed. No work possible that particular day.

Astie had said he'd fill-in a gap in my education, as long as there wasn't any paperwork involved. I'd admitted I was illiterate in the eye-splice. I'd got away without the skill for years. Preferring, I said, a bowline followed-up with a butane back-splice. Everything was man-made fibres so the ends were easily heat-sealed.

By and large, Astie agreed, when it came to ends of ropes. You could forget about crown-knots and stuff when you were working at speed. But an eye-splice was handy. He'd seen a few good knots shaken out by weird conditions. Lost a bit of good gear. An eye-splice was stronger and less bulky. It wouldn't pull out and wouldn't snag so easily.

Catriona had remembered I was coming over. Good timing. The kids were settled and the kettle was on. I passed within their protective concrete blocks. Their roof, like our own, was coping well with the wind from the southwest, coming from the Minches and still blasting through our scheme.

Astie gave me a Swedish fid. With a personal twist to it. Customised, so it was like cheating. Great tool. No, it was mine to keep. They had plenty aboard.

When we'd taken up our samples and spread them out on the settee, I said it was like doing our knitting. Things went quiet. He does knit, she said. A lot of the fishermen do. The Shetlanders are great at it.

And Fair Isle. See all these patterns. Not that different from rope-work when you thought of it. Only a question of diameters.

But the eye-splice is all in that third tuck. Most people don't catch on that the third strand has to go all the way round, before you find a home for it.

And then pull the strands, one by one, tension them back on the rope. See, the rest is easy. You can do them in any order. Four-strand is much about the same. No bother. But wire's tricky. And multiplait. Leave both of these for another night.

Then roll the complete splice under your boot. That's what you want for your mooring or anything that matters. So you don't lose sleep over it on a night like this.

Like the knitting, there's variations. All basically the same principle. Tapering the splice so it'll run through a block. The long splice. Joining two pieces. Strands worked into the pattern of the evening. Droppers off the main rope, linking the creels so the traps will all lie along the bottom.

No creels in this living-room, Catriona said. That was about the only place she drew her own line. She brought a *Daily Record* in with the tea. Caught me with it. Have you seen the *Record*, today? This one was from a date before the century had turned. The print was set even closer than the *Telegraph*'s had been, before the new tech. came. Creases were cracking at the folds.

It was her family story. Some of it was in the printed account. The language was officious, the tone a real irony against today's coloured *Daily Record*, the one my mother had in her living-room.

Nicolson, the Shetlander, was the sole survivor. This was his narrative of a night in 1897, as told to a 'representative':

Cyanus was a fore-and-after, schooner-rigged. She'd departed Bilbao, bound Glasgow. Failed at Ushant. Roderick Johnstone (born on

Heisker or Monach Islands; married in 1837 to Catherine Macleod, daughter of a Stornoway shoemaker; father of two children) sailed as third mate.

From Nicolson, as told to the *Record*:

We should have reached Glasgow last Friday
or Saturday morning had all gone well ...

Off watch, he woke in the night and it was:

... as if the bottom of the ship
was being scraped and torn by crags ...
the Cyanus *was sinking beneath our feet.*

Another named Stornoway man was at the helm. He wasn't found. But Johnstone was identified by initials on socks. Finished with a contrasting colour so the woman who made them would get her man home again.

Catriona knew the rest of the story, more than the *Daily Record*. Her relative, Catherine Johnstone, had made these socks. It was the usual thing. To make them personal. So your man had something unique. Something you could identify. Like the patterns in a fisherman's gensey.

But the family story was, she'd known it, what was going to happen, before he sailed. Roderick Johnstone had been stretching his legs. With his leave nearly up and a deep-sea voyage coming, he'd been out on the moor with his gun. Good for woodcocks and a few grouse, out our way. Standing there, a right tall man, his head bending under the doorway, a bag quite heavy, hanging from his arm. Catherine had seen something.

What did they say? Like that sort of mark around the moon. A halo. The old moon with the new moon in her arms. A reflection. Not even that. Something in the air, alive around him. The last of the light just about going. She was usually quite resigned when he left to join his ship. She did her best. Said all she could. But there was no stopping him, a navigator, by a feeling she had from a shudder in the air.

Catriona folded the newspaper again. Astie checked my eye-splice. Maintaining the sequence of twisted strands. Should do.

I took my test-piece with me to the door. Astie stepped out with me. Just sniffing the air.

You watch this, she said, from inside. He'll be out tomorrow, yet.

Wind was easing. That's all he was looking for. Heavy rain still. I ran for it, back across the court. Looking to see our Yale key, ready in the lock. Hebridean security arrangement.

Redfish

When the silver's dulled by the Grimersta system
the kype's developed
the speckles pronounced
and the belly reddening
it's worth going home via the smokehouse.

Used to be you brought a gill
of dark Aberdonian rum
and additional demerara.

When you get the call, go with cash
and don't forget to take home lemons.
An edge on the blade and the pepperpot primed.
Pour the malt to grant time
for the citrus to do its work.

Che Guevara

I used to fish Loch Langabhat with Che Guevara. Not every day of the week, or even every week in the season but Che and I got out there. At least once a year, for quite a period in our lives.

You'll excuse me if I just call him Che from now on. You might think it's pretentious, even though he doesn't seem to be as well-known now as he was a couple of years ago. When you knew the guy as well as I did anything else sounds silly.

The pressures of organising the revolution hung heavy on Che. Where I come from, trout fishing is a sport of the proletariat. It was logical that rest and recuperation for Che took place on the Long Island. That's the Lewis and Harris one, nowhere near New York, you understand.

Let's also consider the matter of our own town's share in shaping the future. There wasn't much of a plan, but then again we were pretty much opposed to planning in principle. Let's just say there were to be six crofts. Each of the five members of the council would have one and the sixth would have a huge communal barn. Any visitors, wanderers, vagabonds, outcasts, anybody who came across the Minch, could stay there. All our energies were spent in designing this society. So we were far too involved to dissipate energy by digging gardens or cutting peats or going with uncles to fanks at dipping or clipping times.

The discussions took place on the wall opposite the Rendezvous Cafe. You might have thought we'd meet, out of the sun and rain, in the cafe but I was banned from it. OK there was the Lido but Kenny F was banned from there. And Che from the Grillburger. Not a name he'd wish to be associated with, anyway. But we could have had the sense to have all got banned from the same place, so we could collectively go somewhere. Though we put social responsibility to the fore in our thinking, there was, in retrospect, a certain anarchistic tendency. Broke the crust of the pan loaf, bought from a pool of change and ate it just like that, on the wall.

The yeast still seemed alive in the fresh bread, doughy in the centre. It swelled in your stomach when you ate it and you were very aware of it when your mother insisted on you sitting down to the full three courses, some hour or so later.

As to drink, it was wine, after dark. Nothing too middle-class. Fortified, to give energy for the struggle to come. The clash with bourgeois forces when you got back to your own house after eleven, stinking of the drips that had gone from your chin to your jersey. The summers were more sober. But there was one warm June evening when my comrades couldn't save me from myself. Or maybe they were only trying to save the beer. When the Faith Mission had set up their microphone just down from our spot. Somehow I'd bolted, it seemed, from our own congregation and was making a ceremony out of emptying a can of the collective's beer out before them.

Maybe these guys in the suits and shoes, a bit like the Mormon missionaries which were soon to become more common visitors – maybe they had to explain the smell of beer splashed on their gear, when they got back to the Mission. Serve them right for coming up to my house three nights running before they gave up. My mother kept asking about it. The oldman just gave me a hell of a dirty look. I found things to do. Preparations for the first expedition to Langabhat. Good time to get out of town.

It's now clear that Che did as much for our collective as we did to support him. That black hair to the shoulders, that calm presence, at the centre of our group of figures, distributed along these cold concrete copings.

We were all to go, together, to the loch. Two dropped out when they realised how much of a foot-march was involved. Kenny was a casualty of the revolution that very day. The June sun hit his first beginnings of beard. His young head was askew but comfortable on the nets before the fish-market. Seagulls kept a distance off, pecking only at the bits of mackerel and dogfish left in the orange cordage. The bottle was aside on its beam end. The label seems clear to me now, the brand name, one of a few we bought, 365, Lanliq, Four Crown. But all of them with the same legend towards the bottom line: 'Product of the Republic of South Africa.'

What could we do? Kenny F was sleeping, warm in the sun. We couldn't rouse him. We couldn't phone his mother. Between us we didn't have enough money for a cab. The cops were out of the question. Even if we did get him home, he'd only be doing the same in his own bed. So we went fishing.

Getting a lift out of town was never a problem if you were carrying a fishing-rod. I should have remembered that next time I was trying to get out to a dance. A guy dropped us from a pick-up, at the usual departure point for Langabhat. Pity there hadn't been more rain. We wouldn't have much chance of a salmon, yet. Solidarity expressed.

Since, as you will have appreciated by now, this is a story of some historical importance, we'd better get the geography right. Langabhat has Norse origins and means Long Water. There's a loch of this name in the north of the Island, in the Tolsta moor. And in the very south of Harris. But the longest is our Langabhat which is reached from either the Harris or the Uig sides. It's seven miles of inland wet, stretching easily across the dotted line between Lewis and Harris, making a mockery of the notion of borders.

Che and me took to it along the dyke. Enough stones left among the rushes to keep your feet dry. Even in June, you'd go down further than the tops of your boots, if you strayed from that ruined wall. The camping and cooking gear was shared between the two of us. We carried our own rods.

I had the green solid glass fibre job and a Golden Virginia tin of worms. Che had gone to Charlie Morrison's and amongst the sheep-dip and chandlery had found an old, but light, split-cane fly rod by Alcocks of Redditch.

The dyke goes through the saddle between hills. To the north Roinebhal is the rounded top. That's the territory owned by Soval Estate. As you rise towards the sightline, look to the southwest and Stulabhal, with its Himalayan track, winding up it, is in North Harris Estate. The west side was taken by Grimersta and we were on Aline ground. But we went for trout not for revolution that day. Yes, when the rain came and the Grimersta was in spate, the migratory fish would run the whole river, not stopping long in the pools for the paying guests. But this was the dry season. That driver was right, there was no real chance even of a sea-trout.

When your line went tight and a Langhabhat brownie dipped, you knew why you'd come. A clear loch among all that peat. Alkaline balance and sifting gravels. So when you held the rod high the trout would come in, green on the flanks broken by maroon spots, black speckles and glint. Red and green should never be seen. See them on these fish and you want to see them forever.

And the flesh of them, pinked by the freshwater equivalent of krill. Salt and butter on the skin, crackling on a fast burn of heather-roots. Bleached boulders rolled from the lochside to contain our cooking-fire.

You gravitate back to the same part, even with all that shoreline. More than once, Che and I made the walk. What happened in-between these excursions somehow seeming less important in a span of time. But then he and I lost touch. I think his wedding was a key point.

It's not everyone knows Che Guevara got married at all. Still fewer realise that he went through a full Catholic mass in a suburb of Glasgow.

I was one of the survivors of the revolution who made it down. You could identify us, though we'd come from all points of the compass. A scattering of faded jeans, coloured tops, among the suits. Then Che appeared and he was wearing a black velvet suit and a blue velvet bow-tie.

That's a few years back and we could call it quits now. Che could watch me pulling the gear on for work. The polyester tie that clips on; the velcro tabs at the shoulder of the jersey, to take the epaulets of braid which identify my rank. A moderate Republican wearing the crowns of Her Majesty.

Hell, Che, we'll call it all quits. This year I had to reach you again. I knew you weren't a ghost. We had to make that walk. Aline Estate came under New Management. What's new about that? They all change hands when the Property Market is right for it and a lot of the owners never see the places. We've left the middle classes behind now. This toff comes up and blasts a landrover track across the hill. Not our dyke, our saddle but the route south of it, which made the loop. They're sticky about Planning Permission for a shed and greenhouse, if it's near the road, but this guy just blasts through the hill and the hard Harris rock is just left where it falls. You see it from Clisham, you see it from bloody everywhere.

Next thing is, yes chaps you can still fish Langabhat, we realise there has been a precedent. But there are our guests to think of. So shall we say, three chosen Saturdays in the year and we'll have a dram and all that for the heaviest fish afterwards.

The terms weren't acceptable to me. Not to you either. I knew that. So I went for us both. It was later in the year. The rains had come and a trout wasn't enough now. I went to take a fish for us, Che, one that had fed somewhere off Faroes, then returned up over the stones of the Grimersta, home to the loch.

There was a big wind on. I hugged Roinebhal for some shelter and came out closer to the north end of the loch. Couldn't get a line out against the northwesterly so crept up round the top. Into Grimersta territory. There was the run of water out of our loch and still my feet, our two pairs of feet going further down into that territory. Homegoing for me, Che, a steady bearing for the Valtos peninsula. Where my oldman's family had come from before being cleared north.

I cast the spinner into the big water, and did like I've watched them do, on the Ness, the Tay, using the current. My big reel packed-in from lack of use. So I'd to change to the trout reel with the lighter line. When he took me, Che, I knew the weight of the fish from the beginning. One slash with the tail, up like a bloody coal-shovel and he was running.

On his terms, in the big weight of water, so I had just to follow. A sheer gamble. There might be enough of a gale to keep the nouveau aristocracy in their expensive lodge. The ghillies running errands.

Who was I kidding? These people spend a lot of money to act like lords. They'd likely be coming up the loch with the outboard driving, right now.

Still he ran but I sensed the weight of that old green stick, the bend in it, affecting him. The pressure came on till the single strand of mono-filament sang out. He left the water, slashing. I knew I had to lose him but I didn't, Che. He went off again when his fins touched the gravel but next time he came in close.

First, I saw the deep mud-red, the colour in a late male fish. Then he was in the shallow water and I saw him clearly. I wasn't looking at a salmon, Che. It was you on the line. You I was holding. Your straggly black beard out in the flow of the Grimersta. The exact shade of that Che Guevara tee-shirt which gave you your name. The one you wore till the red and black merged. When everyone else was wearing Jimi Hendrix. You clung to it when it was no longer fashionable. Everyone else had moved on to other icons.

congaeel

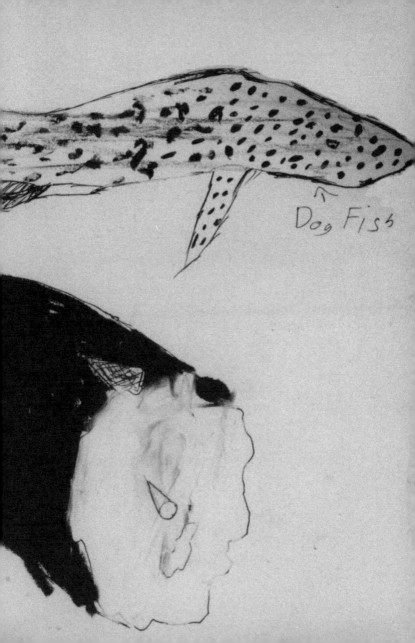

Dog Fish

Afterword

Donald Urquhart

Ten Coastal Recipes

Outdoor Mussels

Driftwood
Freshly gathered seaweed
Freshly gathered mussels

Find yourself a clean coastline. Light a small fire using driftwood and allow to burn until you have a bed of red hot embers. Throw on wet seaweed to cover fire. Immediately place the freshly gathered mussels on top of the seaweed and eat as they open.

Turbot with Pine Kernel Crust in a Red Wine & Chocolate Sauce

Fish with chocolate sounds disgusting but in this recipe it is delicious – trust me. For four . . .

1 large turbot (or halibut)
1 large onion (roughly chopped)
1 large carrot (roughly chopped)
4 thick slices of old wholemeal bread
1 teacup of pine kernels
1 pint of red wine
4 squares of dark chocolate
half a pint of double cream
olive oil
sprigs of fresh dill

Remove four fillets from the fish and skin them. Places the bones, head and skin of the fish in a large pot with four pints of water, add the carrot and onion. Bring to the boil then simmer for one hour to make stock.

Meanwhile, place the bread in a food processor until you have fine crumbs. With the machine still running add olive oil a little at a time until the bread mixture is coated through with oil. Immediately add the pine kernels then the peppercorns then switch off the processor.

Preheat the oven to medium/hot.

Strain the liquid from the stock into a clean pot and add the wine, continue to simmer until reduced to about half a pint. Add the cream then stir in the chocolate and simmer until reduced to a sauce .

As the sauce reduces, place the fillets on an oiled tray, cover loosely with tinfoil and put in the oven for about ten minutes, then remove and discard the foil. Turn up the oven. Place the breadcrumb mix on top of each fillet and pat down so you have an even layer of about a quarter of an inch covering the whole fillet, discard the excess around the sides. Replace in oven until the coating forms a brown crust.

Strain enough sauce onto warmed plate to cover each in a thin layer. Carefully lift each fillet onto the plates. Sprinkle toasted pine kernels around the plate and garnish with sprigs of fresh dill.

Laphroaig Salmon

Farmed salmon should not be used for this (or any other) recipe.

1 side of salmon
3 tablespoons of coarse sea salt
3 tablespoons of demerara sugar
1 bottle of Laphroaig (or any Islay malt)
1 handful of dried dill

Place side of salmon, skin side down, on a tray and check that all bones are removed. Mix the salt and sugar together and add enough whisky to blend this into a paste. Rub this paste over the flesh of the fish then cover with dried dill. Place a weighted tray on top and leave in a cool place. Once a day over the next three days the liquid gathered in the tray should be spooned back over the fish.

After three or four days, during which time the remainder of the Laphroaig may be consumed, the dill and paste should be carefully removed from the fish (without rinsing). Slice as per smoked salmon and serve with pancakes. Garnish with raw salmon eggs (if available).

Benside Prawn Tails

1 full carrier bags of prawn tails straight from the boat
2 bulbs of garlic (chopped)
1 handful of parsley (chopped)
Olive oil

Ask Ian Stephen to acquire prawn tails from a boat coming into Stornoway harbour. In a large wok heat oil and add garlic then prawn tails then the parsley. Toss around over a high heat for two minutes and serve in a large bowl in the centre of the table. Accompany with fresh bread and Highland Park.

Skate Wings in Black Butter
A classic Flemish dish, too delicious for its simplicity.
Per person . . .

1 large skate wing
1/4 lb of butter
juice of one lemon
1 handful of parsley (chopped)
1 small handful of chopped black olives

Place the skate wings in a buttered and place in a medium oven for twelve minutes.

Meanwhile place a heavy, deep pan on a high heat.

Remove the skate wings and place on a warmed serving dish. Immediately drop the butter into the pan – which should be almost red hot. As quickly as possible add the lemon juice to the exploding butter then remove from the heat as you add the olives and parsley. Pour the frothing, dark contents of the pan over the skate wings and serve immediately.

Razor Shells

The hangover cure from heaven.

12 razor shells
1 piece of root ginger
2 tablespoons of balsamic vinegar
half a cup of olive oil
salad leaves

On a clean beach dig out twelve good sized razor shells or, after a storm, pick them up – but they must be fresh and alive.

Place in a bucket of sea water – a bit of sand will improve the quality of their accommodation.

Arrange the salad leaves on a plate. Heat the oil in a wok then add the razor shells, as soon as they begin to open add a couple of pinches of grated root ginger. Continue cooking for a minute or two, shaking the wok frequently. When the shells are open lift them out of the wok and arrange on the salad leaves. Return the wok to the heat and add the vinegar to the oil – immediately pour this hot dressing over the shells and serve.

Green Clam Soup

2 onions (chopped)
2 bulbs of garlic (chopped)
2 pints of cream
2lbs of fresh samphire (chopped)
2 dozen fresh clams
a wee bit of butter
1 nutmeg (grated)

Saute the onions and garlic together in the butter until soft. Add the samphire, stir, then add the cream and nutmeg. Simmer gently for ten minutes. Strain into a clean pot and add the clams. Simmer for a further eight minutes and serve with good bread.

Stuffed Squid Poached in Tomato Sauce

4 large squid
8 rashers of smoked bacon (chopped)
6 large onions (chopped)
1 pint of fresh breadcrumbs
4lbs ripe tomatoes
1 bulb of garlic
Half a cup of olive oil
4 tablespoons of tomato puree

Clean the squid in the usual manner, removing side fins. Keep the main body sacs to one side and chop the tentacles and fins.

In a pan fry two of the onions with the bacon and the squid tentacles and fins in half a cup of olive oil over a medium heat for 15 minutes then allow to cool.

Meanwhile, make a sauce by frying the remaining onions until soft, then add the tomatoes, puree and chopped garlic. Simmer for 20 minutes.

Mix the bacon, onion and squid mix (including the oil) with the breadcrumbs and stuff the squid body sacs with this mixture. Use skewers to secure the top of the sacs closed. Place in an oven dish then pour over the sieved tomato sauce. Cover and cook in a low oven for 2 hours. Serve hot.

Baked Mackerel

Whole gutted mackerel
1 kiwi fruit
1 teaspoon of French Mustard (per fish)
8 fresh tarragon leaves (per fish)

Ensure freshness of mackerel by catching them yourself.

Mash together the flesh of the kiwi fruit, chopped tarragon and mustard and use this to stuff the whole mackerel. Wrap in tinfoil and bake until just cooked. Serve immediately with cold white wine and salad.

Elver Pie

Catch about three pints of elvers in a fine mesh net as they migrate. Keep them alive in a bucket of fresh water and get back to the kitchen as quickly as possible.

3 pints of elvers
1 large onion (chopped)
1 handful of parsley (chopped)
1 knob of butter
1 beaten egg
1 glass of white wine
2lbs of shortcrust pastry

Roll out shortcrust pastry on a floured board until about a quarter of an inch thick and use to line a deep pie dish which has been wiped with butter, cut a circle of pastry to form a lid which will fit the pie dish snugly, cut a small hole in the centre of the lid.

Place the knob of butter, the glass of white wine, the chopped onion and parsley into the pie. Then brush the pastry lid with beaten egg.

Use a sieve to transfer the live elvers into the pie and immediately place the pastry lid on the pie, crimp the edges together to keep them in. Brush the top of the pie, crimp the edges together to keep them in. brush the top of the pie with the rest of the beaten egg.

Place in a medium oven for about 35 minutes after which time the pastry should be golden brown.

Allow to cool and serve cold.

Donald Urquhart

Illustrations Acknowledgements

Thanks are due to the following for permission to reproduce the illustrations in this collection. While every effort has been made to trace and credit the original artists, the Publishers will be glad to rectify any oversights in any future editions.

The children's drawings in this book were developed in workshops that Ian Stephen ran with Fran Stridgen as part of 'North Sea Expressive Arts', an SAC Lottery-funded project working with Aberdeen City and Aberdeenshire Councils. The frontispiece and 'Kingsfish' (pp22-23) drawings were produced by pupils at Victoria Road Primary School, Aberdeen. Pupils from Walker Road Primary School, Aberdeen, made the following drawings: pp 58-59, Kerry Simpson; pp90-91, Daniel Scott; pp162-63, Michael Robertson.

The drawing on pp192-93 came from a workshop with Irvine Young Carers group as part of North Ayrshire Council's Public Arts Development programme.

Biographical Notes

Ian Stephen

Ian Stephen was born in Stornoway, Isle of Lewis in 1955. He worked as a Coastguard Officer on Lewis for over ten years before becoming a full-time writer/artist. His published and recorded works encompass poetry, storytelling, fiction, criticism, and photography. He was the inaugural winner of the Christian Salvesen/Robert Louis Stevenson Award in 1994–95 and has been awarded Bursaries by the Scottish Arts Council. He travels widely to exhibit/perform and to lead workshops.

Donald Urquhart

Donald Urquhart was born in Bankfoot, Perthshire in 1959 and studied Painting at Edinburgh College of Art. He has exhibited both internationally and throughout Scotland and in 1998 received a major award from the Scottish Arts Council. He supprted his early career by working as a chef in Glasgow and continues to cook recreationally at his home in Edinburgh – specialising in fish and game.

Gerry Cambridge

Gerry Cambridge is a poet, blues harmonica player, and a former nature photographer and journalist. He edits the Scottish–American poetry magazine *The Dark Horse*. His books of poetry include *The Shell House* (Scottish Cultural Press, 1995), *'Nothing But Heather!': Scottish Nature in Poems, Photographs and Prose* (Luath Press, 1999), and *The Praise of Swans* (Shoestring Press, 2000). His latest collection *Madame Fi Fi's Farewell*, is forthcoming from Luath Press.

Mike Lloyd

Mike Lloyd has been a radio feature-maker for more than twenty years, producing hundreds of programmes for the BBC and independent stations. He has won prizes in London and New york and has been on the jury of the prestigious Prix Europa in Berlin. He currently works as a freelance producer and journalist.

pocketbooks

Autumn 2001

11   MACKEREL & CREAMOLA

A collection of Ian Stephen's short stories with recipe-poems and children's drawings, *Mackerel &Creamola* is a rich portrayal of contemporary life in the Hebrides, drawing on the author's deep knowledge of sea lore. With a foreword by Gerry Cambridge, recipes by Donald Urquhart, and an audio CD.

ISBN 0 7486 6302 9 paperback, 208pp, £7.99 (including VAT)

12   THE LIBRARIES OF THOUGHT & IMAGINATION

An anthology of books and bookshelves edited by Alec Finlay, gathering an imaginative selection of contemporary writing and artist projects inspired by books, bibliophilia and libraries.

ISBN 0 7486 6300 2 paperback, 208pp, £7.99

13   UNRAVELLING THE RIPPLE

A portrait of a Hebridean tideline by Helen Douglas, this beautiful visual book unfolds as a single photographic image flowing through the textures and rhythms of sand, wrack and wave. With an essay by Rebecca Solnit.

ISBN 0 7486 6303 7 paperback, 208pp, £7.99

Spring 2002

14   JUSTIFIED SINNERS

An archaeology of Scottish counter-culture (1960–2000), edited by Ross Birrell and Alec Finlay. An anthology of poetry, prose, documentation and images featuring Sigma Project, Faslane Peace Camp, Demarco Gallery and the K Foundation.

ISBN 0 7486 6308 8 paperback, 208pp, £7.99

15   FOOTBALL HAIKU

An anthology of 'Football Haiku' published to coincide with the 2002 World Cup in Japan and South Korea. Edited by Alec Finlay, with photographs by Guy Moreton and an audio CD.

ISBN 0 7486 6309 6 paperback, 208pp, £7.99 (including VAT)

16   LABANOTATION

Alec Finlay's celebration of the Archie Gemmill goal, Argentina World Cup, presented as a dance by Andy Howitt. Studio and stage performances photographed by Robin Gillanders, with labanotation of the goal.

ISBN 0 7486 6325 8 paperback, £7.99

Available through all good bookshops.

Book trade orders to:
Scottish Book Source, 137 Dundee Street, Edinburgh EH11 1BG.

Copies are also available from:
Morning Star Publications, Canongate Venture (5), New Street,
Edinburgh EH8 8BH.

Website: www.pbks.co.uk

Mackerel & Creamola

An audio CD

Material collected and recorded by Ian Stephen 2000-2001

Contributors (in order of appearance):
Ben Stephen; Gerry Cambridge; pupils of 1st Year, The Nicolson Institute; Daniel (Irvine harbour); Irvine Young Carers; Jimmy Budge ('Lassie story'); Mary Smith ('The Little Hind'); Home-Educated Group (Irvine Area); Rab and Gus (Scottish Maritime Museum); David Middlemiss (guitar aboard *Josh*); pupils of Cliasmol School, Harris; Ally Macleod ('Reef dogfish story').

With thanks to the participants.

Edited and mixed by Michael Lloyd.
Produced by Michael Lloyd and Ian Stephen.
Manufactured by Key Productions, London.

Contact: miklloyd@hotmail.com